The Serpent Dance

The Serpent Dance

SOFIA SLATER

SWIFT PRESS

This paperback edition first published 2025
First published by Swift Press 2024

1 3 5 7 9 8 6 4 2

Copyright © Sofia Slater 2024

The right of Sofia Slater to be identified as the author of this Work has been asserted by her in accordance with the Copyright, Designs & Patents Act 1988.

Typesetting and text design by Tetragon, London
Printed and bound in Great Britain by CPI Group (UK) Ltd, Croydon, CR0 4YY

A CIP catalogue record for this book is available from the British Library

We make every effort to make sure our products are safe for the purpose for which they are intended. Our authorised representative in the EU for product safety is Easy Access System Europe, Mustamäe tee 50, 10621 Tallinn, Estonia gpsr.requests@easproject.com

ISBN: 9781800752573
eISBN: 9781800752566

For Trixie Chalevant

Dhe'n gwer yn hans kerthys'vy
Ha'n gorthewer tek dhe'm brys;
Yn le may whelyr mowysy,
Ow quary dro tansys.

Curunys yu my metheven,
Mar gough gans y wyluen;
Dres pup pras ha blejyewen'
Gans whekter a dhenew.

…

Yn boreles war'n glaston-ma,
Aga hus a ransons y,
Erbyn dos dewyn kensa,
Ha'n jeth ow colowy.

                    As I walked out to yonder green,
                            One evening so clear,
                All where the fair maids may be seen,
                          Playing at the bonfire.

                    The bonnie month of June is crowned
                          With the sweet scarlet rose,
                    The groves and meadows all around,
                          With lovely pleasure flows.

                              …

                    All on the pleasant dewy mead,
                      They shared each other's charms,
                    Till Sol's first beams began to play,
                      And coming day alarms.

FRIDAY

CHAPTER 1

With hindsight, she could see that the whole set-up was an invitation to bad luck. They wouldn't be able to get away for their first anniversary – that fell during a major new install at Noah's gallery – and he wanted to make it up to her. So they were popping the champagne a little early, with a long weekend away after ten months together, location to be revealed.

Never celebrate something before it's happened.

At the time, though, she'd been excited, and happily set about proving to herself that they were, as she hoped, going to Paris. It was the obvious choice: within easy reach of London, and full of museums – trawling through museums and galleries already being how they spent most of their weekends. She'd never been, in spite of how close it was, and Noah knew it was on her bucket list. She found the epithet reassuring, too: the City of Light. No night-time panics likely there.

Not that she'd voiced this to him explicitly. But she'd dropped hints. And he'd smiled knowingly every time she teased him about the surprise, clearly certain she'd be happy with what he had planned. She was sure it was Paris, and, for a few weeks, she spent the time she should have been working on illustrations for the new book staring out of the window instead, blind to the bus stop and the overflowing bin that made up the view. She saw instead her and Noah feeding each other little forkfuls of something buttery at a bistro, their table overlooking a cobbled square. Her and Noah crossing bridges arm in arm, while an accordion played faintly in the background. Her and Noah being visibly in love. Paris would make it obvious. Paris could make it certain.

She couldn't get to sleep the night before they left, and stayed up late double-checking her passport was in date and trying to decide which little silk scarf would look most French when tied around her neck. She chucked a fresh sketchbook into her bag too; lately she'd been a little lazy about keeping her sketch diary. All the drawing she did was for work, and she was feeling stale. Paris would surely refresh her creativity, with its gorgeous architecture and decadent food, not to mention the Louvre, the d'Orsay and all the romantically bare garrets once home to artistic greatness.

Still dreaming of oozy cheese and floodlit churches, she woke early. A last check of the luggage, a last look in the mirror. A faint hope that she'd have transformed, overnight, into someone who looked the romantic part. But no, hers was still just a presentable face: dishwater hair cut in a fringe, hazel eyes, cheeks tending to the round. Ah well. Beautiful or not, someone was still taking her to Paris for the weekend.

Noah picked her up in a cab, and she leaned in for a long kiss, blushing a little when he looked bemused. She wasn't usually one for public displays of affection. But the taxi turned west, not north towards St Pancras, and a faint shadow of misgiving fell over her heart. 'Where are we headed?' she asked Noah.

'Patience, patience,' he replied, coy, still playing the romantic game. She tried to smile back, to keep the flirtation going. But when they got out of the cab at Paddington and Noah pulled two tickets to Cornwall out of his pocket with a flourish, she couldn't help but feel crestfallen. She could tell from the disappointment in his face that the disappointment in hers was hurtfully clear.

Settled in their seats on the train, she tried to improve the atmosphere, chattering as she unpacked the sandwiches he'd bought, cheerfully reading out crossword clues. But her heart wasn't wholly in it. The truth was, she hated the countryside, and she resented Noah for not knowing this. Also, she'd put so much effort into believing what she wanted; she felt stupid, and resented him for that, too. She might have been happier with Cornwall if she hadn't expected Paris.

Noah must have been able to sense the insincerity of her smiles, because he barely responded to her, just yanked the culture section out of the paper and fixed his eyes on the reviews. Audrey watched from the window as London petered out around them, and, remembering last night's excitement, felt a tiny bit like crying.

Occasionally, with Noah, there were these... *gaps*. They'd met ten months ago, both swiping to match, and at first she'd felt wildly lucky. Finally life seemed to be turning into what it was always meant to be. He was ostentatiously good-looking, with high cheekbones and glossy dark hair that fell over his forehead. She started sketching that perfect face now, in the margin of the paper, cross-hatching a shadow to bring out his full lower lip. It was sometimes a source of worry, the distance between them in this regard. He was markedly beautiful; a little skinny maybe, but that fit the part – an art world denizen, stick-thin and draped in beautiful clothes – whereas Audrey had long ago admitted to herself that she was entirely average. Which wasn't to say she couldn't brush up nicely. But her prettiness ebbed and flowed depending on things like her mood, the time of the month or the effort she'd put in on a given day, whereas she'd never been out with Noah and not seen someone, man or woman, checking him out. Nevertheless, he seemed to find her plenty attractive, and the sex was good. Good enough, anyway.

And they had plenty in common professionally. They might be playing in different leagues, but the sport was the same. Noah worked in a big-name gallery, the kind where he and all his colleagues wore black and got invitations to private views and VIP openings at art fairs and museum retrospectives. Audrey toiled at the more commercial end of the art world, in graphic design and illustration. It had been the practical option; she had needed to make a living straight out of university and had started freelancing several years ago while she was still a student on the sensible, useful graphic design course her parents had pressured her to choose over art college. There had been no funds and no time for experimenting or waiting-and-seeing-how-things-go, but she'd never let go of her childhood dream of being an artist. A real one. Who drew and painted things because they haunted her head, not because a textbook needed a diagram of the kidneys, or a new restaurant wanted a logo.

She couldn't deny that the world Noah gave her access to had been part of his attraction. At the start, she'd pictured them together at all those private views. He'd introduce her to his colleagues, and they'd laugh together over wine, and she, too, would be dressed in black and wearing interesting jewellery. Maybe, eventually, she'd show him some of the work she did for herself in her spare time, and he'd be amazed, and want to show her at the gallery, and her whole life would be different.

So far it hadn't worked out like that.

He did take her to gallery events at first, and she did drink the free wine, but she never seemed to say quite the right thing; his colleagues gave her thin smiles and found ways to leave the conversation. Most of the time, Noah didn't want to go to openings. 'Done one, done them all,' he said whenever she asked. So now they spent more evenings in than out, with a takeaway and the telly. Like anybody, Audrey thought. But she wanted to be somebody. When she'd dug what she thought of as her 'dark drawings' out of a drawer and showed him, he just nodded slowly and then turned to the commissioned illustrations scattered across her desk, picked one up and said, 'I love this, though!' It was a drawing of a dodo.

That wasn't a problem. It wasn't that she wasn't in love with Noah. He was the handsomest man she'd ever get the chance to be with. It was just... these little gaps.

And, oh God, there it was, on the train, that stupid dodo, staring at her from across the aisle. She prayed Noah wouldn't notice and fixed her eyes resolutely on the fields, cows, hedges, fields which had repeated endlessly since they exited the London sprawl.

'Look, Audrey, it's your book!'

She gave a tight smile to acknowledge he'd spoken, but said nothing in reply. Her turn not to play along with his attempts to cheer her up. He was oblivious, or pretended to be.

'Excuse me. Excuse me? My girlfriend illustrated that book,' he said, leaning across the aisle, gesturing at Audrey and giving a full-wattage smile to the mother who was holding the book open, pointing out the different animals to her toddler. All he got in return was another vague smile and nod. She was clearly more concerned with keeping her kid quiet than with meeting the book's creator.

'Stop, it's embarrassing,' said Audrey in an undertone.

'What did *The Times* say? "Equal parts urgency and enchantment"? Baby, it's brilliant. You should be proud!'

'I was just working to a brief.'

'Come on! Every time I see that dodo, it makes me smile to think you drew it.'

She shrugged and turned back to the cows, hedges, farms, fields. Noah raised his hands in a little gesture of exasperation, and the strained atmosphere descended again. When she was sure he was looking away, Audrey began to obliterate the drawing she'd done of him next to the crossword, scratching it out one heavy line at a time.

He had quoted correctly. *Equal parts urgency and enchantment.* The book, a children's compendium of extinct species, had recently been released and was selling unexpectedly well. With barely any text, just the names and death dates of a series of animals, along with a few facts about each, Audrey's illustrations had been given all the credit for its success. She thought it was more down to humanity's rising ecological panic than her drawings, but the upshot was more attention for her work than ever before.

The trouble was, it was the wrong kind of success. She tried to see it like Cornwall: the problem was her expectations, not the situation. There were definitely perks – she liked having money in her pocket for the first time – but she also felt further than ever from the serious artist she'd always dreamed of being. Everyone now thought of her as a charming children's book illustrator. Once you had a reputation, she worried, it wasn't easy to rewrite it.

Then, too, there was something hollow about success when you didn't have anyone to share it with. She had Noah. Except it never quite felt like they were on the same hilltop together, taking in the same view. Her family: better not to think of them at all. And most of her friends, she was beginning to realise, were really acquaintances whose congratulations meant little to her. The more praise the book received, the more she felt alone.

The project had been a last-minute commission when the first illustrator dropped out, and she'd dashed off seemingly hundreds of dodos, thylacines and great auks in a matter of weeks. She'd enjoyed herself, but it was just another job, another number of pictures to get through. Now that it had done so well, they'd signed her up for a second one, a kind of atlas of endangered Britain, from hedgehog to hedgerow. Those drawings had been due last week, but she had yet to even begin, and her publishers had started asking her when they'd see the first drafts – politely so far, but with an unmistakably anxious frequency.

She had told Noah how she felt, but there again, a little gap had appeared.

'What's so wrong with success?' he'd asked.

'It's not about success, it's about identity,' she'd replied. 'It's how I want to be defined. I'm always going to be that girl who drew the cute dead animals.'

'Grass is always greener. The up-and-coming artists I work with would kill to have some cash and name recognition. You should be grateful!'

She hated it when people told her she ought to be grateful. Even when they were right. Gratitude seemed to be an emotion you never felt when you were meant to. Like this trip; Noah had arranged everything, paid for it all. And all she felt was disappointment.

They pulled into a station: Exeter St David's. She stared out at the crowds shifting and waiting under the green platform roof. Maybe she should just get out here and head back. It wasn't only the disappointment and the strained atmosphere that were getting to her. It was the knowledge that the sun would go down and there would be no streetlights to mitigate the dark. In the countryside, night was night.

Noah had never complained about her leaving the blinds open while they slept. It was one of the reasons she liked him.

But he'd probably been oblivious. And she hadn't exactly wanted to make things explicit. *You know how small children need night lights? Same deal.*

She'd spent too long thinking about it, and now the train was pulling away from the platform. Looked like she'd have to put up with a couple of dark country nights. She didn't want to admit how uncertain she was that she could endure them.

After Exeter, she forced herself to make an effort.

Tea arrived, dispensed from a cart pushed by a man in a green waistcoat. She ordered two, and two slices of fruit cake wrapped in plastic, handing one to Noah with a conciliatory smile. She pushed croissants dipped in café au lait from her mind. As the man handed over the cardboard cups, some of the scalding water leapt out from an insecure lid, splashing over Noah's fingers. He winced and she reached out, dabbing at his hands and clucking in concern. 'You okay?'

His hands closed around hers and she looked up to see him smiling at her, his perfect smile. She returned it, sincerely, for the first time since they had got on the train.

'So tell me about the place we're going.'

'Deepest, darkest Cornwall.' She tried not to wince. 'Some village near the south coast. They have this midsummer festival, left over from pagan times, a really authentic celebration, you know? Costumes and bonfires. You're always talking about how dull the country is.'

'So you wanted to prove me wrong?' She said it lightly, giving him the chance to take it as flirtation. His smile indicated that he had. But once again she was disappointed: of what she'd shared of her childhood, he'd retained only the word 'dull', the sense that she'd fled boredom, nothing darker. Stop it, Audrey, she told herself. She'd never made it more explicit, so he couldn't be expected to understand. And yet didn't love mean crossing that gap sometimes, being able to understand things even when they weren't spoken?

Then, something extraordinary. The train broke out right next to the sea wall, running parallel to the shore only a few metres away. The waves must come right up to the tracks in a storm. Out on the sun-sparking water, sailing boats tipped this way and that. Red rock outcrops thrust up along the beach, and between them families were engaged in a laughing struggle against the breeze and the gulls, arranging rugs and umbrellas, protecting their picnics. It was beautiful.

'Is this why you think I should get out of London more?' she asked, nodding at the panorama.

'Magical, no?' He flashed The Smile. 'I came once as a kid. I never forgot it.'

'So we're recreating a childhood holiday?'

'Not exactly. My parents and I stopped in Devon. We're going further.'

She tried to imagine wanting to return to any of the scenes of her childhood. Noah was adopted, something he'd told her without looking her in the eyes; there was hurt there. But from the sound of it, his parents were lovely people, kind and generous. They'd supported him for his first few years in London, letting him figure out what he wanted to do. She hadn't said, *It's not always worth knowing your real parents.*

'Where'd you hear about the festival?' They were pulling away from Plymouth now, crossing into Cornwall. The sea wall was far behind them now, the endless roofscape of the city's terraced houses all that was visible from the train.

'Oh, just around, you know.' He waved his long-fingered hand vaguely, suggesting a swirl of information in the air, waiting to be seized. His knee was juddering, she noticed, and the hand, once it had completed its gesture, descended to tap an anxious rhythm against the moulded plastic of the table.

'You seem kind of edgy. Is everything all right?'

'Just impatient. Hate trains. We're getting close.'

'Should I be nervous too? You said this festival had pagan roots. Will I have to climb inside a wicker man when we get there?'

He didn't pick up on the joke. 'It's actually wicker animals here, not wicker men,' he said earnestly.

Noah seemed distracted for the rest of the journey, tapping fingers and feet, staring fixedly out the window. They weren't that close yet; there was still the change to a branch line ahead of them, over an hour to go. In the silence, it occurred to Audrey that she ought to let someone know where she'd be all weekend. She'd let herself get carried away with the idea of Paris, and had told everyone like it was a certainty. But when she got out her phone to send a text, there was no service. Ugh. The countryside. She turned to the window and shut her eyes against the strength of the summer sun, trying not to think about how she'd feel after it went down.

CHAPTER 2

There was a taxi waiting for them at the station. But a taxi without a driver isn't much good. They stood next to the parked car, looking around with a mixture of hope and impatience. 'Are you sure this is the one you booked?' asked Audrey.

Noah didn't appreciate the question. Of course he was sure. *Trevennick Taxi*, it said, right there on the side. Silence fell, the same miserable-but-not-admitting-to-it silence that had prevailed on the train. Noah stood tapping his phone in a private bubble of exasperation. So they wouldn't be sharing this trouble. Fine. Audrey waited for him to resolve the mystery and gazed around at the station and its environs. Only a few passengers had got off here, all greeted and driven away. Now the roses and pansies in tubs along the platform were nodding in the heat, their rhythm slowing as the air stirred by the train's passage went still. Audrey traced a few lines in the pollen and dust on the taxi's windscreen: swipe, swipe, dot, squiggle, and she'd made a snake sticking out his forked tongue at the scenery.

The station was tucked into a little cleft between hills. Trees crowded dark on each slope. A bent iron gate gave access to the nearest wood. The reclined angle and patches of rusty moss told the story of a long, losing battle with time. The trees behind the gate grew close, blocking all the light; Audrey couldn't imagine anyone choosing to walk there.

Here the heat was heavy, far heavier than it had been in London, and loud with bees and birds. She could feel it descending on her, as thick and yellow as the pollen on the car. She could almost fall asleep here, leaning against the taxi, watching those woods behind the gate. They needed watching. Something looked liable to slither out of the shadows, into her dreams. She stared deeper into the trees. The shadows looked wrong somehow. As though they were darker than they should be. Or greener. She took a step forward, for a better view. The dark behind the gate seemed to bulge slightly as she stepped towards it. The way it moved seemed unnatural. Like the snake she had just drawn had leapt into being and was writhing slowly through the hot dark.

A door slammed behind her, and she jumped and turned at the sound. 'They take their time down here, I guess,' said Noah with a tight smile at her, as though she'd been the one sighing and chafing at the wait.

The station cafe was in a little hut perched above the platform, and now a man was coming down the stairs, raising a hand in their direction. The taxi driver, she supposed. She looked back at the forest. Nothing. Too long staring at the passing scenery from the train must have tired her eyes.

Now she took stock of the driver as he came towards them, unhurried. He was black, with shaggy hair rusted gold here and there by the sun. About the same height as Noah, he was equally well endowed as far as cheekbones and full lips went, but with an easier smile and very different clothes: a loose old shirt and jeans, worn in and faded like his curls. Nothing like Noah's precise trouser cuffs and expensive wool sweater – wasn't Noah hot in those? Next to the man's heels a broken-coated dog the colour of bleached straw was trotting, tongue lolling in the heat.

Nearing them, the man stuck out a hand. 'I'm Griffin, hi.'

'We're going to Trevennick,' said Noah, ignoring the hand. 'I booked. Did you get the time wrong, or decide to stop for a coffee?'

'More of a tea drinker really,' said Griffin, smiling at Audrey, who dropped her gaze. 'But no, I work in the cafe there, just needed to shut up shop.'

'Right, well, shall we get going?' said Noah, unmollified.

'Don't worry, village'll still be there.'

Audrey was grateful she was still looking down; it made it easier to tuck her smile out of sight. When she looked up, Griffin had noticed the snake she'd drawn on the dusty windscreen, and he smiled at her when she blushed.

Into the car: bags piled in a muddy boot, and an apology for the dog hair. The dog itself went in the front seat. Again, Audrey had to suppress a smile as Noah began fastidiously picking hairs from his long legs while the dog stared back at him with an open, panting mouth. She felt a bit disloyal.

Then they were away, hurtling down steep-sided lanes. When they had to pull into a passing place to let someone by, Audrey spotted small purple flowers and heavy-headed grasses growing from the stacked stone walls. Then, off again. They were rattling over roads full of sudden dips and steep climbs; the breeze through the windows was a relief in the heat, but the speed and the stone walls pressing close to the car were frightening. Where the stone gave way to hedge, twigs whipped at the open windows and scraped at the doors, small reaching cousins of the menacing wood. Audrey hoped every turning was the last, but the alarming drive continued.

'So you're down from London then?' asked Griffin, eyes on them in the mirror as they whipped round a sharp bend.

Audrey, clenching the door handle, managed a 'Mm.'

'Staying in the big house?' Still his eyes were on her in the mirror. It was a bit worrying; she could see a tractor coming.

'Is it that big?'

'Size matter to you?' His grin got bigger as he said this, still looking into the mirror, not at the road. He changed down a gear and pulled out of the tractor's way just in time. It rumbled past, twice as high as the car and carrying some sharp silver attachment on the back, whose many points jutted at them through the window. When they were under way again, he gave a more direct answer: 'It's not enormous, but it's where the local squires used to live, in the days when there were such things. Lots has changed since then, but round the village we still call it the big house.'

The village began to gather but took a while to cohere. A farm stood proud of its steep fields; over the next rise a few houses were strung along the descending road. Griffin had slowed now, and Audrey had time to take in the houses, some withdrawing into the trees, built half into the hillside, like caves that had acquired a civilised front. There was something secretive about the landscape, all those buildings standing apart from each other, tucked into slopes and woods. Everything was made of stone and had small windows. She thought of the farming families who had lived in such places a century ago, cut off from everything but the land, isolated behind their thick walls. If something went wrong behind walls like that, how would anybody know?

She shivered, and as she was shivering, she spotted the snake and nearly screamed. She immediately felt silly; it was only a sculpture, stood by someone's garden gate. And she was in a car! What harm could it do her? And yet she did feel obscurely harmed, or, if not harmed, vulnerable. As though the snake – a creature she had just doodled, had thought she'd seen in the woods – had been placed there as a message to her specifically. We see you, it said. But this was stupid. She was tired and out of her comfort zone. It was nothing but a garden decoration, some bit of village hall arts and crafts. It was about shoulder height, woven out of thin branches. The word *withies* popped into her head, but that might be wrong; she was no outdoorswoman. They drove on and she tried to put it out of her mind.

A few garden gates later, there was another sculpture, of a curly-horned ram. And then two more a bit further along, a horse and a bird, though the bird looked slightly wrong, as though it had borrowed some of its parts from a fish. She supposed withy wasn't a medium that allowed for much accurate detail. Still, the strange bird was a bit unsettling, the way a child's drawing sometimes ends up accidentally ominous. Despite the heat and the little beads of sweat standing on her lip, she felt a shiver. She cleared her throat. 'Those animals…'

'You mean the obby osses?' replied Griffin. They must be for the festival Noah had mentioned. The blonde dog stared back at her, panting hugely as though laughing at her. She was being ridiculous.

But before she could finish reassuring herself – or ask what 'obby oss' meant – there was the grind and screech of the taxi as Griffin pulled to a sudden halt.

A commotion in the churchyard. Among the yews and gravestones, a man and a woman stood arguing. There was a yellow haze to the air from the heat, pollen and road dust. The thickened distance seemed to slow and distort their shouts and gestures. She felt as she had looking into the forest, only now the confusion was caused not by darkness but by light. The shadows cast by the people in the graveyard weren't behaving as they should.

'Tain't right,' the man said, while the woman, red-faced, reached up to grab his strident hands. He thrust her away angrily.

'Oi, Trev,' called Griffin. 'What's up?'

The man had been facing away from them, but as he turned, she saw why Griffin had intervened. They were obviously brothers, though Trev appeared to be a few years older, and a good bit surlier. His lips curled into a snarl, rather than a smile like Griffin's.

'Drive on, Griff. 'Sall right.' He was controlling himself in front of strangers, but his chest was rising and falling quickly.

The woman's eyes darted nervously between Trevor and the taxi. She called out, in a voice strangled by forced cheer, 'Have you got the Trevennick House visitors there? Welcome to the village! I'm Lamorna Pascoe.' She gave a little wave. Her expression was worried, embarrassed, but not rageful like her companion's. Her thin blonde hair, cut to chin length, was sticking to her cheeks in the heat. She was all in black, and, Audrey now noticed, wearing a dog collar: the vicar.

Griffin hesitated, but then another car pulled up behind, braking sharply, and the driver leaned out to shout at them, 'You're gonna die!'

'What did he just say?' asked Audrey. The driver had a thick accent; she was hoping she'd misheard.

'He's suggesting I learn to drive.' Griffin stuck his hand out of the window in a placating gesture; after another jerk of the head from his brother, he put the car back in gear and pulled away. Audrey turned around, and saw the pair watching the receding taxi. The sun was behind them, and she could only see their dark, hazy shapes.

'Wasn't expecting a welcoming committee,' said Noah, drily.

'First time there's been paying guests up at the big house,' replied Griffin, in an absent tone that indicated his mind was still on the argument they'd witnessed. 'Talk of the village, you are.'

Audrey and Noah shared a look of discomfort at this idea. Immediately she felt better. That little glance of complicity reminded her that they had been together a year – well, nearly – for a reason. She liked him. They belonged to the same world. The gaps were bridgeable. She was annoyed that her eyes kept meeting Griffin's in the rear-view mirror.

Now they were past the church, the village began to gain mass and density. A couple of smaller streets wound up the hill away from the river. The houses were side by side here, but they still had the isolated look of the scattered farms; the tiny windows set deep in stone walls had an ungenerous air, like they were designed only for looking out, never in. It was a sunny summer afternoon, but all the buildings seemed to retreat into damp green shadow. They rumbled over a narrow bridge and passed a pub, a post office, a village green. Here at least it was open enough for the afternoon light to spread itself around. On the grass, people were standing and building something out of the same materials that had been used for those midsummer creatures. They stopped what they were doing and turned to stare as the taxi drove past. Audrey wondered if the whole weekend would be like this, everyone watching wherever they went.

The village was all old stone and mossy roof slates, twisty corners and climbing roses. Audrey thought of the brief for her follow-up. How had Jemima at the publisher's put it? 'Something about the vanishing creatures of field and hedgerow, you know, Beatrix Potter but with science, a piece of English nostalgia for kids who've always been online.'

As they passed through the village, she took mental snapshots to sketch later – this setting was exactly what they were after, though she'd have to brighten it up, make it charming. She supposed she *should* find it charming. But it felt... hostile.

They pulled away from the houses, following a road parallel to the river, which climbed higher as the channel cut by the water deepened. The river widened as they went, heading towards the sea, becoming more clearly an estuary; she could see plastic buoys bobbing orange in the water. But the forest hadn't given way. Trees crowded close here and on the opposite bank. Even rushing past in a car, she didn't like to look into the darkness between their trunks.

Still, the place was beautiful. The sun bounced off the water in fat, slow slabs, and bronze reflections slid around on the river's surface. The birds were the only things in the whole scene moving in any kind of hurry. Seabirds, she thought, all winging inland with swift determination, though the shore was a few miles distant. She went to point them out to Noah, but as she did so she noticed his face and fists, both clenched. He stared out of the window with tense and avid eyes, scanning the water and the treeline, as though they were withholding something from him.

'Are you all right?'

His response was slow, and more than a little false when it arrived. She watched him unball his fists, work his jaw loose, apply a smile. 'I'm great! Just looking out for spots I recognise.'

'Sure?'

'Yeah. So excited to be here.' He kept his head turned forward for the rest of the drive, mastering himself, ignoring the landscape. She kept quiet. But something troubled her: hadn't he said they stopped in Devon on that childhood holiday?

Griffin seemed to sniff the air. He found her again in the mirror. 'Storm's coming,' he said, cheerfully.

The house, when they reached it, was not at all what Audrey had expected. The picture-postcard village, the sleepy scenery, the heavy afternoon with its feeling of sinking into a layer of dust, plus the fact that everyone kept calling it the big house: she'd prepared herself for a centuries-old confection of many wings and starched green lawns. Mellow bricks, a gravel drive; somewhere you could set a bonnet drama.

But in fact the place was a modernist shock, all angles and glass. Like many of the older houses they'd seen on the way, it was half set into the hillside, with woods crowding it towards the riverbank. Here it wasn't even a bank but had become steep and high enough to count as a cliff. You'd not survive a fall. Unlike the other houses in the village, though, this one was almost completely open to the light. Huge slabs of glass tilted this way and that to make a many-faceted shape, like the rocky hillside continuing itself in new materials. You could see inside, and there too everything was open, rooms flowing into each other as the building withdrew into the hill.

They got out of the car and stood, looking at the transparent building, the woods, the cliff falling to the river. For the first time all day, Audrey felt pleased with Noah's surprise. 'Wow,' she said, and he turned and smiled broadly, naturally. She felt silly for all the resentment and disquiet she'd been nursing. It was going to be a wonderful weekend away with her getting-serious boyfriend. Certainty was there for the grasping.

Then two things soured the moment.

First, there was a clap of thunder, and, looking west, she saw why those birds had been heading inland: a dark front of solid cloud, marching sternly towards them. Griffin had been right about the storm.

Then a woman emerged from the house, moving fishlike through the aquarium effect of all that glass, distorted by ripples and reflections. She stood smiling at the front door, waiting for them to come to her.

But Noah didn't move.

Audrey looked at him. His face was stricken, almost horrified. Under the fading rumble of the coming storm, she heard him whisper, 'Oh fuck.'

CHAPTER 3

He quickly plastered a smile over his dismay. 'Hi, we're Noah-and-Audrey, we're renting the place this weekend,' he said, sunnily. Audrey was comforted by his practised rhythm. She could rest her doubts in his certainty. Still, she heard an inner note of disquiet, rung first by his upset and now by his quick recovery. He ignored her searching look and moved forward, hand outstretched, false smile secure. 'I made the reservation with Cameron. That's not you, is it?'

But he knows who she is, thought Audrey. Else why that reaction?

The woman raised her hand to shake his. Audrey inspected her, and found her somehow familiar. She was short and buxom, with pale messy hair piled on top of her head. She carried herself with assurance, and dressed like she considered herself no less attractive for being middle-aged. The slow lift of her hand, the one-sided smile, the time she took to respond – everything suggested a high estimation of her own value. A woman who felt herself to be in her prime. 'Cameron's my assistant, but he's away at the moment. I'm Stella Penrose. I own the house.'

They stood there, joined hands slowly pumping up and down, for a beat longer than necessary. Audrey broke the silence. 'It's an amazing place.'

Stella shifted her gaze and took Audrey in for the first time but didn't relinquish Noah's hand. Audrey hefted a bag, to remind everyone why they were there. In the distance, thunder rumbled.

Stella finally turned to lead them back inside. 'You'll want to freshen up after your journey.' Noah followed without even looking at Audrey, and it was left to her to settle the taxi fare.

'Your man been here before?' asked Griffin, searching through his pockets for change.

'No.'

'Huh. Seemed like he knew her. Bit of an atmosphere, wouldn't you say?'

Now Audrey was irritated. He wasn't wrong, but what business was it of his? 'You can keep the change,' she said, with as much frost as she dared, and stalked off. But there he was, keeping pace with her to the door, carrying the other bag, which Noah had left her to deal with, and smiling broadly, like her hauteur had amused him.

'Very generous. And just so you know, Stella can be a bit difficult to swallow. If you get sick of her, there's decent food at the pub.'

Then he was off, and the car was out of sight back down the hill before Audrey could think of a cutting reply.

She stood at the door, trying to settle herself. Sure, the impudent taxi driver seemed more concerned with how she felt than her boyfriend; sure, said boyfriend was being strangely withdrawn and was obviously hiding something from her about why they were here; and sure, here was the last place Audrey wanted to be. But it was going to be fine. The problem had been her expectations.

And her expectations had been surpassed by the house. It really was amazing. Stella would show them around, then she would leave, and once Audrey and Noah were alone, she could figure out what was going on with him. This weekend could still be everything she wanted it to be.

The rain started, and she hurried herself and the bags indoors.

They had moved further into the house, but it was easy to find them. Once again Audrey thought of a fishbowl: Stella and Noah were rippled, fractured, partially obscured by intervening layers of glass and furniture. They were in what must be the kitchen. Stella, short, with her greying blonde curls loosely gathered on her crown, and Noah, tall and dark-haired, stood on either side of a kitchen island, apparently engrossed in a murmured conversation. Audrey made her way slowly towards them, duffel bags banging into her calves, looking at the house around her as she went.

She proceeded down a central hallway with a stone floor that seemed to have gathered all available cold into itself. On either side were... what? Living spaces, she supposed you would call them. They couldn't quite be called rooms, open as they were to each other. The spaces were divided not by walls but by sofas, folding screens, side tables and waist-high bookcases stuffed with volumes. At first she thought the corridor was walled in with glass, but then she realised the transparency was that of air. The pictures marching at eye height down the hall's converging perspective lines weren't fixed to anything, but cleverly from the ceiling, their frames back to back, one image facing this side, one facing the other. She leaned in to look at one of these: an etching, eighteenth-century by the looks of it, men in stocking caps lolling drunkenly over barrels in some sort of cellar. She leaned back, and noticed the picture swaying as she moved the air around her. There was something disconcerting about the lack of walls. As though she might wake up tomorrow and find it all changed, nothing firm in the world around her.

In the kitchen Noah was explaining his work, talking about the gallery. He was sketching pictures in the air, describing the exhibit they were installing next month, the one that meant they couldn't go away on their anniversary.

'Pencil drawings, incredibly detailed but on a massive scale, so you get this fascinating micro–macro interplay. We're calling the show *Good on Paper*.'

Stella laughed, a throwing-the-head-back kind of laugh which Audrey decided had taken practice to develop. Noah, handsome as he was, tended to have that effect on people. Still, she felt a twinge of jealousy – why was he telling this stranger details he hadn't yet told her? This was the first she'd heard of the exhibition's title.

When she spoke, her tone was more peevish than she'd planned. 'Where can I put the bags?'

Stella pulled her gaze away from Noah's gesturing hands and looked at Audrey, a little coldly, she thought. Was it coldly? Something about her face was bothering Audrey. But her smile was brilliant. 'Of course! You must want to see your room.'

They walked past a dining table and chairs – another space defined only by the furniture – and came to a door, where Stella paused. It was made of glass, of course.

'This is the master bedroom.' It was beautiful, with a high bed, a glass wall partitioned into levered windows, and beyond that: air. You could see across the estuary to the trees, their green muffled by sheets of rain streaming and pooling on the glass.

'This must be right on the edge of the cliff,' said Audrey. 'It's like living in the sky.'

Living luxuriously, too: the bed was huge, and covered in the kind of linen sheets that were always rumpling their way across lifestyle magazine features. There were a few pieces of low wooden furniture for clothes and things, understated but, judging by their fine grain and invisible joining, obviously custom-made. Among the blue-black mussel shells and desiccated white starfish skeletons decorating the top of the dresser, Audrey spied a half-open jewellery box with glittery depths. Stella spent a moment showing off the view, naming escarpments, pointing out that the only human intrusion on the landscape was a line of round orange buoys which indicated mussel ropes, bobbing where the estuary widened.

'When you think this was just another dull old country house – and not even a very impressive one – until the last squire knocked it down and rebuilt it in the 1960s. Of course, it's a pity the family were ruined by the expense. Overambitious. But then, as someone who lives in a glass house, I shouldn't throw stones.' The head laugh again. Definitely studied. And Audrey was betting that joke reappeared every time there were visitors. 'Anyway, this is where I sleep, and you'll be in this room here,' she continued, moving them along to another glass door.

This room, too, was beautiful, as was everything in the house, though the bed was less imposing and the view of the crowding woods less exhilarating than the huge vista that filled the master bedroom's outside wall. But what was niggling at Audrey wasn't that they were being fobbed off with an inferior view.

'You mean, you're staying? While we're here?' Noah winced as Audrey spoke, but she was too dismayed to find a more tactful way to ask.

'Well, yes, I live here. But don't worry, I don't bite.' She looked to Noah and added, 'Not hard.'

All day Audrey's hopes for the trip had dipped and rallied, but this felt like too much – sharing a largely transparent house with a head-laughing stranger who was making coy sexual comments to her boyfriend. Entering the room, dropping her bags, she sat heavily at the foot of the bed.

'I'll leave you to settle in,' said Stella. 'Bathroom's that way.' She walked off, the wooden soles of her clogs resounding against the stone floor.

'Do you think the bathroom has a door?' Audrey asked. Noah had come in and was standing with his back to the wall of trees, the rainy grey light silvering his outline, his expression a little obscured by shadow. She could tell he was tense; he was working his hands, as he had already so many times today.

'I'm sorry if the place isn't up to your standards.'

He didn't sound sorry but resentful. She sighed. For a moment she'd hoped that the strange atmosphere building between them all day would break. If he wasn't about to open up and tell her why they were here, or why he was acting so strangely, they could at least share an eye-roll at the situation. But he seemed determined to be obtuse.

'It's not what I was hoping for, I'll admit. I mean, this house is amazing. But you know I'm a city mouse. And why did you reserve somewhere where the owner would be staying with us? It doesn't exactly make for romantic seclusion.'

'I guess I got it all wrong.' Still the refusal to see what she was getting at. Now Audrey felt irritated as well as despairing.

'But why did you want to come here? Is there something going on? The way you've been looking around since we got to the village, like you're trying to find something. And do you know that woman?'

'I don't know her, but don't you recognise her? She's that telly historian. Stella Whatsername.'

This brought Audrey up short. That explained the sense of familiarity that had been worrying at her mind's edge since they arrived. She remembered the programmes now – those curls blowing around in the wind on top of Hadrian's Wall or Glastonbury Tor, while Stella declaimed that this, or this, or this, was the real heart of ancient Britain. Nothing she'd ever watched, exactly, but she'd caught moments here and there while flicking through channels. Suddenly she felt silly, and oddly nervous. She'd been so argumentative, so confrontational; had she ballsed everything up with Noah because she couldn't place a TV presenter's face? And beneath that anxiety, a more disloyal question: was he really so stunned by minor celebrity as to react the way he had? Her cherished image of him was more worldly than that. 'Penrose,' she said. 'Stella Penrose. I – I guess my mind ran away with me a little.' She moved closer to him. 'Noah, you've been distant all day. I was looking forward to it being just us, on this trip.'

'Sorry I didn't try hard enough to please you.'

'Come on, of course that's not what I… Look, I'm sorry.' He was staring stonily out of the window as rain lashed against it. Thunder rumbled in the distance. She kept going. 'The place is beautiful, and I'm grateful for all the planning you did.' Noah shrugged, with an air of modest acknowledgement. 'Can we get some time alone, though? Let's go down to the pub for dinner.'

'Look at it out there. We'd need an ark. And besides, Stella invited us to eat with her. We can't really say no.' He turned and left the room, ending the conversation. Audrey stifled a sigh of frustration and let him go.

She looked around the room; she'd been too upset to take much note of it at first. In the corner, she now saw, was another one of those wicker sculptures. This, too, was a long and sinuous snake. It didn't have eyes; none of the creatures did. And yet it seemed to watch her as she moved.

CHAPTER 4

At least Stella was a good cook. There was a large fish on the table, giving off fragrant steam and surrounded by a halo of sliced lemons. The wine was buttery and crisp, better, Audrey imagined, than anything they would have found in a backwater pub. The rain drummed on the glass roof, and the table felt like the one light place in a watery, darkening world. She tried not to think about the moment when full night would arrive.

'So, Audrey, Noah's told me a bit about his work, but what is it that you do?' Stella was neatly parting the white flesh of the fish, apportioning potatoes, passing around plates. This could actually be fun, Audrey thought. When else have I had dinner with a minor celebrity?

'I'm an artist. Of sorts.'

'She's being modest. Audrey's a very successful illustrator, she's just had a big hit with a children's book.'

Before dinner, Noah had taken an extremely long shave, locking himself in the bathroom as he did so. Audrey had been left stewing on the bed, staring at the snake staring at her, slowly getting furious. But this seemed like a peace offering.

'A picture book, how sweet.'

Audrey bristled at the condescension. She might acknowledge to herself and her boyfriend that things weren't turning out quite as she hoped, but that didn't mean she wanted a stranger belittling her success.

'It's got quite a serious message, actually. It's a compendium of extinct species.'

'But don't you think it's terrible the way they dumb down these important themes? Every time I'm in a bookshop, I see the words-to-pictures ratio has shrunk yet again.' Stella's fork hovered in the air. 'It's the same with my books, of course. It used to be that we'd have one plate section in the middle with images. How many do you think we had for the tie-in with my last series, *The Thistle and the Rose*?'

'Four?'

'Four. Yes.' Stella made a slight face, as though Audrey ought to have said nothing at all – the question was rhetorical, and she'd ruined the punchline. 'Four!' Stella said with renewed emphasis. 'And they made me pay the permissions. But then how many do you think we sold?'

Audrey didn't bother to reply; she was beginning to recognise Stella's habit of supplying the answer as well as the question. She let their hostess go on bragging and watched her turn the beam of her attention back onto Noah.

They seemed to get on well. Stella was an admirer of Noah's gallery. Noah, apparently, was an admirer of Stella's programmes. Audrey ate the irritatingly delicious food and listened to them talk.

'It was coming from this area that first kindled my curiosity about the past,' Stella was saying, misty-eyed. 'Like all out-of-the-way places, it's preserved little pockets of history intact. Old ways, older legends.'

'I saw those statues in town,' said Audrey, observing the difficulty Stella had in pulling her gaze away from Noah's face. He was, after all, very handsome. 'Woven out of branches or something? They kind of creeped me out.'

'Very good, Audrey.' Is she going to give me an actual gold star? Audrey wondered. But no, just a lecture. 'That's the sort of thing I mean. We call them obby osses, from hobby horse, obviously, since they're often horses. Or snakes or rams, they take various forms. It's a very old tradition, a kind of propitiation of local gods. We build them every year at the Feast of St John, or Golowan, what's called midsummer "up country". Then there are offerings to the river and a bonfire on the village green – protecting ourselves from flood and fire and dragons and pestilence, you know.'

'Dragons?' Audrey asked, with a kind of laughing disbelief. 'Isn't that a little medieval?'

'You may be surprised, but no,' said Stella, still in presenter mode. 'In fact it's much older than that. Animals have always been a repository for our fears and an expression of our powers. Especially dragons and snakes. Think of the ancient carving of the river goddess Verbeia at Ilkley, holding her two serpents.' Stella stuck out her elbows, as though she were the goddess.

It was difficult for Audrey to think about the river goddess Verbeia, because she had no idea what Stella was talking about. But her role was not to respond, it was to nod slowly and thoughtfully while the expert held forth.

'That's why you must throw your obby oss into the fire. It's a mystic release of their power. Previously it was real animal bones, you know, bone fire, bonfire. But modern pieties have defanged our traditions, more's the pity, and now we have to make do with wicker.'

Audrey felt relieved, picturing herself lobbing the wicker snake in her room onto a bonfire. Stella continued.

'There's an old example in your room, actually. It's terrifically bad luck to hold on to them, but I just couldn't resist. It was a very special Golowan for me, back when I was a young woman.' Though she had begun her monologue speaking to Audrey, she was facing Noah again by the time she concluded.

'Can't be very old at all, then,' he said. The head laugh made another appearance.

Oh my God. Was the flirting mutual? It was hard to interpret it any other way: Noah's gallantry, Stella's coy laughter. She was used to people trying it on with him, but Noah didn't usually seem that interested. She'd always trusted his loyalty, until seeing him with this woman.

Audrey inspected her rival, half hostile, half curious. It was true she wasn't old: just past fifty, perhaps. She wasn't a strikingly beautiful woman, but she acted like she was, and this was almost the same thing. She was always shaking that messy hair back, adjusting her clothes, jangling her jewellery. Drawing attention to herself; happy to be looked at. Audrey might have some youthful advantages of face and figure, but she could see which, of the two of them, had the charisma for telly. Whereas I have what? she thought. A face for radio?

'So you're from here then?' Audrey asked.

Noah looked down at his fork, turning it on one side, then the other. Like he was patiently waiting to have Stella back to himself. Did they wish Audrey weren't there?

'Yes, originally. Though in quite different circumstances. Over the years, I've lost the accent and gained this little place.'

'Sounds like there's a story there,' said Audrey.

'Oh yes. A long story. For another time,' Stella replied. Then, immediately ploughing on: 'It involves a tall, dark man, very good-looking and very disreputable.' Noah leaned in, looking keen to hear it all. Audrey regretted asking.

Dinner dragged on. And on. At least it did for Audrey. The other two seemed to be enjoying themselves rather a lot. Stella sparkled; Noah seemed enthralled. It was odd to see him like this – he was normally aloof, firmly ensconced in his reserve of cool. Maybe this was what he was like at work, around the prominent artists the gallery showed. Gushing and attentive. He was never like that with her. Audrey silently put back glass after glass of the good wine. And then, all of a sudden, she was drunk. 'Do you always rattle around in this big place alone?' she asked Stella, reaching for the wine bottle again and slopping some of it round the base of her glass as she poured.

Stella smiled thinly. 'Not usually, no. Cameron lives here too.'

Audrey found it odd that they were renting a room out, given that both Stella and her assistant lived here and, in spite of the size of the place, it only seemed to have two bedrooms. Had she and Noah supplanted this Cameron person in his own bed?

'The assistant? That's all you have for company?'

'In future I think I'll have more.' A warmer smile, directed at Noah. My God, they really were flirting, right there in front of Audrey. But Stella carried on in a different vein. 'I've got big plans for this village – it needs developing, it's been allowed to languish too long. Things have to grow to survive.'

'Here's to the future, then.' Audrey raised a wobbly toast. Noah smiled tightly, embarrassed. She found this grimly satisfying, and knocked back another glass. Might as well keep going; she was in it now. But it was one drink too many. Suddenly the spotlights over the table were glaring in her eyes. Her head pounded and the next time lightning flashed outside it made her feel dizzy. She stood, a little unsteadily, and announced, 'I'm going to bed.'

Noah nodded acknowledgement, but didn't make a move to join her. Stella, with a little smile curled in the corner of her mouth, watched Audrey stumble off to the bathroom.

Let them sit there chatting away into the night, then, she thought. She brushed her teeth and changed into the silky nightgown she'd packed for the trip, snorting derisively at herself. It definitely wouldn't be needed tonight.

She should draw before she went to bed; it was her habit, her way to unwind. But she'd been blocked lately, and now she was drunk and wrung out. She sacked off drawing, and lay in bed as the rain washed down the wall of windows, trying not to look at the dark trees, occasionally made vivid in a flash of storm light, and trying not to listen to the cosy murmur of her boyfriend being chatted up.

Audrey felt sick and sorry for herself. Paris would have been so much nicer. For one thing, no creepy old snake sculptures in a Parisian hotel. *It's terrifically bad luck to hold on to them.* As she slipped between sleep and wakefulness, the snake sometimes seemed to writhe in the dim, shifting light of the storm. And all the time, she couldn't shake the feeling that it was watching.

The murmur from the kitchen seemed less cosy now, more impassioned. Audrey couldn't hear what they were saying, between the distance and the rain, but she was sure Noah's voice was raised, almost in protest. Had he led Stella on too far, and now he was trying to fend her off? If the open plan of the house didn't make discretion impossible, she would get out of bed to creep closer. As it was, she lay there, straining to hear, until the rumble of talk died down again and faded into the drumming of the rain.

Noah was in the room. She must have fallen asleep; she hadn't heard him come in. He was there, in the corner of the room, next to the basketwork snake, hopping around as he tried to get out of his trousers. Audrey felt some of her anger dissolving at the undignified sight of him. She giggled and he turned to face the bed.

'What?'

'You look like you're in difficulties.'

But Noah wasn't ready to be friends again. He jerked himself out of his trousers and into his pyjamas without replying. Beyond him the house was mostly but not entirely dark – she could see light which must be emanating from Stella's room, though the intervening distance and the position of the bed prevented her from seeing directly into the room itself. Faint noises told her that their hostess, too, was changing for bed.

'How was the rest of dinner?'

'Delightful.' He got in under the duvet, still moving brusquely, making his displeasure obvious.

'You two seemed to get on.'

'We did. But even if we hadn't, I would have made an effort to be polite.'

'You think I wasn't?'

'You got drunk, were passive-aggressive and walked off before pudding. I felt I had to hang around to make up for you.'

She couldn't deny that this was all true. And yet at the time it had felt like she was the one being baited, ignored, wronged. But then she had drunk a lot of wine. Had it all been petulance on her part, a wilful misinterpretation of perfectly normal behaviour?

'What was pudding?'

'If you wanted to know, you should have stayed and eaten it.'

Not taking the proffered olive branch then. Audrey could feel her anger, quickly soothed, just as quickly reawakening. She lay on her back clenching her jaw and staring at the ceiling – not glass; this part of the room was buried in the hillside. Noah pettishly tucked the duvet around himself, as though to demarcate a border between them.

'Crème brûlée.'

'What?'

'Pudding was a crème brûlée.'

'Well, at least that's one thing that would have been the same in Paris.'

'Paris? Is that where you thought we were going?' He sounded genuinely surprised.

'It's where I hoped we were going. Clearly my hints needed to be more obvious.'

'If you care about hints so much, you should get better at taking them.'

'What the hell does that mean, Noah?'

'Nothing. You're pissed, and I'm trying to go to sleep.'

'That's not it.'

'What do you think it is then?'

'I think you're being weird. I think we came here for some reason other than to celebrate our anniversary.'

'Such as?'

'I don't know, do I? You haven't spoken to me properly since we left London.' She could feel his back tensed against her, his knees and arms drawing into himself. She took a breath and decided she didn't have anything to lose. 'I'm beginning to think maybe you brought me here to break up with me.'

That at least got him to turn over. 'Who books a holiday to break up with somebody? That's insane.'

'Is it? You've been ignoring me all day. You spent all evening flirting with some woman you just met tonight.'

'You've got the wrong end of the stick. That's not what's going on at all.'

'Well then, what is?' She was on the verge of tears now, her voice coming out raw.

'I just…' His hand came a little way towards her over the duvet, and she hoped that he might explain. But when he spoke, it was only to say, 'This is all in your head. We're here to have a nice time. For our anniversary. That's it.'

She could play along with his pretence that it was all fine; that she was imagining things; that they were Noah-and-Audrey, a happy young couple having a lovely time. She probably should play along if she wanted a chance of having if not a lovely, then at least a tolerable time while they were down here. But she didn't want to pretend. She wanted something real. So she kept going. 'Is it because she's on telly?'

'If that's really what you think, Audrey, maybe we should break up.'

'Seriously?'

Noah sat up. 'You haven't exactly been great company all day. Look, I'm sorry this isn't the trip you'd have booked. Okay, so the location was a mistake. Next time we'll go to Paris. And okay, I thought it would be fine that the host would be here, because it's a big house. But I didn't bring you here to break up with you, I was trying to do something nice. Maybe you're the one who wants to break up with me.'

'Noah, come on…' Now she was pleading, trying to cover the fear that he'd called her bluff. Had she fabricated an excuse for a row to try and get him to do the breaking up? He was nice, and he was handsome, and they had chemistry. But did she love him? Or was she just trying to close the gap between her idea of what she wanted and the reality of how it felt? She gripped her eyes shut and tried to ignore the

thought of him describing the new show. *Good on Paper*.
'I wasn't trying to—'

'But you did.' He sighed. 'Look, let's talk tomorrow. I don't have the energy right now.' And he turned away from her again.

She lay there with Noah's hostile silent form on one side and the dark trees on the other. She listened to the rain, and thought about what she should have said differently, and tried to unpick the tangle of hurt and confusion and rage. There was still a light on somewhere in the house, but looking out of the wall of windows, she was staring into blackness. She could feel herself suffocating, drowning in it. The snake in the corner, a darker shape against the dark, stuck out its forked wicker tongue in mockery. She'd never get to sleep.

Then, with a start, she woke up. It was still dark, and Noah was standing by the bed. Something had startled her – not him, but she didn't know what it was, and now he was leaning over and shaking her. 'Get up,' he hissed. 'I think something terrible has happened.'

CHAPTER 5

Because of the peculiarities of its construction – largely made of glass, and dug into the hillside – the house was all on one level. One might have called it a bungalow, had it not been so striking in design, so full of fine pictures and precious objects.

Audrey had already observed on entering that the space was largely demarcated by furniture and suspended pictures. Here a cocktail stand proffered sociability, there a preponderance of books indicated a sort of study. The house had the same shifting personality as a stage, defined by props and the performances that went on there. But nature was the only audience, pressing greenly through all that glass.

Further into the house, greater concessions had been made to the necessities of domestic life. The bathroom, she'd been relieved to find, did have a door, and opaque walls too; some of the forest-facing view had been sacrificed to build them. The walls and fittings were built of the same trees that could be observed in their living state outside the house. Audrey still remembered enough about tree identification from a childhood in the Girl Guides to notice this. It was silly really: she hated being away from civilisation, but she couldn't forget knot-tying or the proper method for starting a fire in the rain.

She had also noticed the frightening way the branches of the trees tapped and caressed the large bathroom windows while she was readying herself for bed. Noah and Stella had still been sitting in the kitchen, in their pool of lamplight and complicity. Beyond the kitchen were the two bedrooms at the back: Stella's large one, facing the river, and the slightly smaller one where they were staying, facing the woods. Between the two rooms was a gap, with a Persian carpet covering the flagstones. The gap extended into the hillside a little way, making room for what Stella had indicated were cupboards. Even a house like this needs a hoover, Audrey supposed.

The beds themselves were positioned both to make the most of their respective views and to create a bit of privacy, with the headboards turned away from each other across the gap. There were also filmy curtains, made of lichen-coloured watered silk, which could be pulled for more discretion. It was possible to dress or undress without the details being observed – though a silhouette might be visible through the thin green fabric. But it was impossible to move about the house unseen, to enter or exit a room unobserved.

All in all, it was the least private house Audrey had ever entered. If it hadn't been in such an isolated position, displaying its inmates only to birds, woods, and river, it would have been a scandal. But the layout made it easy to be sure of one thing: there had been no one else in the house with them that night. It was just Audrey and Noah. And Stella, dead on the floor of her room.

She was on her back, blood pooled around her, a knife in her neck, her hand on the knife. She hadn't pulled the curtains, so they could see her clearly through the glass, illuminated by her bedside lamp. She had changed into pyjamas, and the yellow silk of her top – the left shoulder now stained a deep red – was bunched up, exposing her naked stomach. It was undignified, and Audrey felt sorry for her, laid bare like that in her last moments.

Audrey couldn't go and straighten her clothes, or even check for a pulse, though, because the door was locked from the inside. She and Noah stood outside, rattling the door, staring through the glass, stunned.

Shocked as she was, Audrey couldn't suppress a petty reflection that this wouldn't have happened if they'd gone to Paris. Aloud, she asked 'What happened? What the hell happened?'

But Noah was frozen, staring, and didn't respond to her question. Audrey suddenly fizzed with energy, terrified energy. She couldn't stand still looking at the dead body for another second. She walked over to the tall standard lamp, taller than a person, which arced over the kitchen table, and turned it on. As she did, she thought she heard footsteps echoing on the flagstone floor, and her heartbeat, already dizzyingly fast, sped up. She stopped and listened, but no other sound came. It must have been her own movement;

perhaps she'd knocked against something. It was hard to feel the normal limits of her body; or to keep track of time; or to think. Experience was coming in flashes, as though every moment she was just waking up.

She walked through the entire house, switching on every light she could find, trying not to look at the darkness outside, the gesturing branches, the flowing river. Soon the whole place was ablaze. If you were watching it from the river or the woods it would seem like a stage, set in the darkened theatre of the night. She tried to shake off the feeling someone was watching.

Audrey returned to Noah, still petrified in front of Stella's door. This time she shook him; she couldn't wait any longer for him to snap out of it. 'Why would she do this, Noah? Why would she kill herself while we were in the house?'

'She can't have. She wouldn't have.'

'But she did. Look, it's only us here.' As she said it, she felt her heart lurch at the possibility she was wrong. She stalked over to the bathroom, threw open the door, rustled the shower curtain. She came back and opened every cupboard in the little recess between the bedrooms. They were too low for a person to stand in, anyway, and so full of cleaning supplies and cardboard boxes that no one could have crouched there. They were alone. It was just them. And Stella.

Suddenly, Audrey thought of Noah standing over her in the dark. She looked at him. He seemed shell-shocked, broken. Would you seem stunned like that if you had just done something terrible? Maybe.

'She wouldn't have done it, she—'

'Why were you awake?' she interrupted. Slowly he focused on her, gathering a response. She thought – or hoped – it was shock, not the pause of a planned lie.

'I heard a bang. Really loud. I couldn't sleep after our row. And then her light came on, so I thought I'd look.' He started weeping quietly, wiping away the tears with the heels of his hands like a child. It was strange, the difference in their reactions. Audrey felt like a wild animal, sinewy and buzzing with fear. And he was so... weak. Too weak to kill, surely?

The locked door. She rattled the handle again. Still locked. From the inside. She could see that the bolt had been brought across under the handle. And it was Stella's hand on the knife. She had taken her own life. She must have. But she hadn't seemed like the type. Hours before, she had seemed greedy and pleased with herself, a cat licking cream from its whiskers, not someone who wanted to die. And why invite strangers to your house if you were going to commit suicide?

Audrey paced up and down, trying not to look at the body. 'The police! The police. Have you called the police?'

Noah shook his head, still crying. She was sure now he'd done nothing to the dead woman, and she felt a little sorry for him, a little tender. He was panicking, breathing raggedly. She led him to the dining table, sat him in a chair. Her phone still didn't have reception, but there was a landline. She called. A suicide, she said. They'd send a car, there was a policeman in the village, he'd be there in a few minutes.

The rain settled into a steady downpour, but there was no more thunder or lightning. They sat in the bright house with the stormy darkness all around them, and listened to the rain on the glass. Sitting there, feeling the dark outside the house and, in a different way, inside it, she couldn't calm her heartbeat. She tried pacing up and down. But she knew what she needed to do. She went to their room and grabbed her sketchbook, and took up a position outside Stella's room. Her hand hesitated over the page; was this a terrible violation? Probably. But when she looked over at Noah he hadn't noticed, he was just hunched and crying. She had only herself as a witness, and she needed this, she needed to record it, to turn life into lines. It was what she did. What she had always done when something terrible happened. If she sat there opposite him she would go mad.

She made a mark on the paper, and then another, and she kept drawing, occasionally shifting her position to see the body from a new angle, or looking beyond the body to the objects in the room, until the police arrived.

CHAPTER 6

A resonant knocking on the front door. Audrey left Noah collapsed into himself at the dining table, and made her way towards it.

She could see a man peering in through the glass, hands cupped against the pane, his raincoat pulled up awkwardly to protect the nape of his neck. He smiled broadly when he saw her coming, which she found odd, in the circumstances. 'You wouldn't call it dry, would you?' he said when she let him in, stamping on the mat and flapping his arms to shake off the water.

Audrey stepped back slightly, out of range of the spray. 'Is it just you?' she asked.

'They're sending more along from Falmouth,' he replied. 'But I live in the village. This is the first time it's been professionally convenient. DI Paul Morgan.' He stuck a hand out and she shook it, a little hesitantly.

'Shouldn't you have backup or something? What if you're heading into danger?'

The broad smile returned. He looked her up and down,

and she felt terribly conscious of her silk nightie, only half-hidden by the sweatshirt she'd thrown on top. 'It's kind of you to think of it, but they called in a suicide. Not usually much danger from a suicide.'

She felt wrong-footed by his levity, so she said nothing, simply turned and led him into the house. DI Morgan sighed and snuffled as he went. He was a large, ungainly man, his clothes sitting awkwardly on his body, a button missed here, a hem untucked there. He'd probably dressed in a hurry, but his clothes looked like they fit badly at the best of times. All in all, he didn't fill her with confidence. She realised how much she'd been looking forward to passing this problem to someone else, someone responsible who could take it off her hands and leave her free to depart and forget she'd ever seen this place. But she wasn't sure DI Morgan was that person.

At the door of Stella's room, he stood looking for a few long minutes. Eventually he turned and said, 'Neither of you went in?'

'The door's locked,' replied Noah, lifting his head momentarily from between his folded arms. DI Morgan looked at him, with a much more serious face than at the door, for almost as long as he'd looked at the body. Then he nodded and extracted a tool from his pocket, with which he picked the lock, giving them a little grimace as he did so. Audrey wasn't sure whether it was apologetic or proud.

When the door opened, Audrey smelled blood, rolling out from the room in a warm metallic wave, and she had to sit down next to Noah.

The detective entered the room carefully. Once again, he simply stood looking for what seemed a long time. He changed position occasionally, squatting down on his haunches, considering the dead woman from this angle and then that. Audrey watched him through the glass, thinking guiltily of how similar she must have looked, drawing the body. Thank God Noah hadn't seen that. Next to her he kept his face buried in his folded arms. She considered reaching over and rubbing his back, but she didn't. It was strange that they hadn't hugged each other since this happened, or offered each other any comfort. Or not so strange, given the fight they'd had before they went to sleep. The argument seemed more significant, given that even the sudden intrusion of death hadn't wiped it from her mind.

Eventually the detective reached out, checked himself, got a latex glove from his pocket and pinched it between his forefinger and thumb, then used the protected grip to push Stella's blood-soaked pyjamas away from the wound. He brought his own hand across his body to the base of his neck, as though re-enacting the fatal movement. After this he stood, turned and crossed to the window, looked out and, with a fresh glove, tested the latch.

When he emerged, he shook his head a little and said, 'I don't know about this at all. Awkward way to do it. But I don't see that it can have been anything else. Terrible for you two. Down on holiday, aren't you?' Audrey nodded. 'And neither of you knew her?'

Audrey shook her head, then looked at Noah. She tried to keep expectation and curiosity out of her face, but she felt both. He looked back at her for a moment – a long moment, she thought, forcing herself not to turn her gaze to Morgan. She wondered whether he, too, registered the pause.

'No,' said Noah finally. 'I mean...' and here Audrey's heartbeat quickened, thinking that circumstances might at last force him to be honest, to explain how they knew each other, because she was sure, absolutely sure, she now realised, that Noah had known Stella. But all he said was, 'I'd seen her programmes on telly.'

'Ah yes.' Morgan rocked back on his heels, calling up a memory, then splayed out his hands and spoke in a booming voice, evidently quoting. 'Beneath these hills lie secrets, wealth and the history of the world, all contained in one malleable and shining metal: tin.'

'I... didn't see that one,' said Noah.

'Too bad, too bad, it's a good thing to know about down here, tin, very important. In fact, mining is at the heart of—' But before he could go on to explain more about tin mining to his bewildered captive audience, there was another knock at the front of the house. Backup had arrived.

This man, his dark uniform shiny with rain and his eyes heavy with interrupted sleep, was introduced as Sergeant Varley. There were more coming behind, he said, to photograph the body and bag up evidence. He was younger than Morgan but a tidier and more serious presence than his superior officer, more the reassuring figure of authority Audrey had been hoping for, though it was still Morgan in charge of the scene. The DI asked Varley for his assessment, and he stood at the door of Stella's room, looking over the body. Then he proffered, with a slight hesitation, as though anxious to get the answer right, 'The angle's awkward. It's the wrong grip.'

The broad smile returned, and Morgan clapped his hands together. 'Excellent, Varley, you'll make detective yet.' Then he turned to Noah and Audrey and explained. 'The way she's holding it is alright for stabbing yourself in the heart. But she hasn't done that. I wouldn't want to stab myself in the neck, and nor would you, but if you did, you'd want to make it quick and easy, wouldn't you? Or would you?' Morgan mused on the mysteries of the suicidal mind.

It was an odd thing to say – surely the police were meant to keep information and supposition to themselves? But behind the glitter of conspiratorial bonhomie there was something watchful in his eyes, like he was gauging their reactions. They all waited, until Audrey began to wonder whether the question hadn't been rhetorical after all.

'Well, what do I know? At any rate, in spite of the funny grip, here she is. She was in a locked room, locked from the inside, that is, and she was found holding a knife, with the blade embedded in her neck. As there was no one in the house but these two…' Something occurred to him, and he looked keenly at Audrey and Noah, still sitting side by side at the table like naughty children. 'There was no one in the house but you two, was there?'

'Just us,' said Audrey. 'And I think we would have noticed.' She gestured at the open-plan house, its glass walls.

'Not discreet, is it? You checked the cupboards, the bathroom and everything?' He smiled indulgently as he asked this, as though he knew, of course she had, a clever girl like her, but he had to make sure. She nodded, and he said 'Good,' but he sent the sergeant to open every closed door anyway. There was still no one hiding in any of the very few hiding places offered by the house.

Once his words had been proved true, DI Morgan carried on, suddenly brisk and organised. 'As there was no one in the house but these two, and as there is no other egress from the room, the window giving on to a cliff, and as the deceased was found holding the instrument of her own death, we have no choice but to conclude that we're dealing with a suicide. Would you agree?' The sergeant, who had slipped into an open-eyed doze during this summing-up, righted himself and nodded vigorously. His superior gave him the indulgent smile of greater experience, and said, 'You'll get used to nights, Varley, never fear.'

If Noah had been alert, she might have shared a glance with him, wondering at the informal ways of the rural police. But he was almost in a stupor, just about able to rouse himself to answer direct questions, sunk in some horrified inward contemplation the rest of the time. Is there something wrong with me? wondered Audrey. Should I be that stunned too? Or is there something wrong with him?

The sleepy sergeant went to let in the rest of the police team, and soon there were half a dozen people in disposable blue shoe covers, letting off photo flashes, taking their prints, itemising the room the body had been found in and making the whole thing look a bit more professional. DI Morgan nodded his satisfaction at this activity, then extracted a notebook and asked Audrey if she knew of anyone else who'd been in the house recently.

'We only saw Stella when we arrived this afternoon. But she said her assistant lived here too. I don't know when he went away.'

'Cameron Grant?' replied DI Morgan. 'He left for his stag yesterday morning. Didn't she say? Those two were getting married.'

At this, Noah's head popped up from the table, and his eyes looked more sharply focused than they had since finding the body. 'Married? She was getting married?'

'In a matter of weeks. Make a fine couple, too. Lovely heads of hair, both of them.' DI Morgan waved his hands around his head to suggest a mane, then caught sight of the body on the floor and dropped his arms. 'Well, made a fine couple. Poor man. What news to come back to. And he'll probably be hung-over to boot.'

Noah, jolted out of his shock, now seemed angry. His jaw churned and his dark eyes were bright again. Audrey, too, felt a little infuriated – she didn't care whether Stella was marrying or not, but if Noah was this upset about it, then he hadn't been honest with her during their fight. Some flirting must have been going on. She crossed her arms and glared at him, grumbling internally about dissembling and obfuscation, until she realised DI Morgan was speaking again.

'And are you two heading that way yourselves?'

'Which way?'

'To the altar.'

Audrey was unable to stop herself snorting. 'I don't think so.'

'Audrey...' Noah's tone was pleading, his eyes too.

'Been arguing, then?' DI Morgan asked, with a sharpness she wouldn't have credited him with.

She would have liked to rehash their row, precisely because it would embarrass Noah, but she caught his anxious gaze and thought about how it looked, the two of them hostile and angry, the dead body in the house. 'Just a tiff at the end of a long day. You know how travel takes it out of you.'

'Not when you have such a charming travel companion, surely?' said DI Morgan to Noah. But Noah had sunk back into his own thoughts as soon as Audrey had backtracked about their fight, and it was left to her to respond. She ignored the gallantry. Or was it sarcasm?

'We just had a few words before we went to sleep. I was expecting to stay in a hotel. Look, this has all been... horrible,' she said. 'Do you have everything you need? I'd like to go home.'

'Ah, now. I can understand you wanting to leave, spoils the holiday a bit, doesn't it? But I'm afraid it'll be best for you to stay in the area for a while,' replied the detective. 'Of course, we'll find you another bed, but we may have further questions about this business, and we wouldn't want you having to come all the way back from London just to answer a couple of little queries. Just for a day or two. Most likely.'

Most likely. So he was suspicious. They could do nothing but assent.

The DI said he'd leave the scene to his team and drive Noah and Audrey into the village to find another bed for the night. They'd barely unpacked; it didn't take long to gather their things, though they had to submit to a search. A gloved Varley pushed Audrey's drawing supplies this way and that, opened her travel toiletries and gave them a sniff. He shook out her sketchbook, saw nothing fall from between the leaves, and was about to start flicking through when a pair of lacy pants (utterly pointless now) distracted him. He lifted them on the end of a pen, the sketchbook still in one hand.

'I think that's all that's necessary, Varley,' said DI Morgan, giving the embarrassed Audrey a fatherly smile. The search was over before the other policeman could even move on to Noah's bag. Audrey was relieved; she hadn't fancied explaining her drawings of Stella's corpse.

They stepped out of the door, flinching against the still-heavy storm, and Morgan guided them to his car. The house looked even more like an aquarium in the rain, with the ambulance's blue light flashing on it.

Morgan shook his head gently. 'Such a strange thing. Not in a million years would I have taken that woman for a suicide. But it sometimes happens around Golowan, you know. A bit of madness in the air. The river must have its due.'

CHAPTER 7

Audrey was glad it was wet, though she got half soaked stowing her things in the boot before they drove off. The headlamps glinted off the rain, and the river sent up a million silver flashes. Being outside in full dark, coming on top of everything else, would have sent her into a panic.

She sat in the passenger seat next to Morgan. Noah sat in the back, staring out at the night, angry, turned inward. In a way it was like their journey to the house. Moody, quiet. Only the unspoken questions were different. Not *What's going to happen to us?* but *What did happen between you?*

'You'll be staying at the vicarage,' said DI Morgan, steering down the curves of the hillside with long, slow turns of the wheel. 'I called and told the Reverend Pascoe to prepare for you.'

'Is there any need to put her out?' asked Audrey. 'Doesn't the pub have rooms?' She framed it as polite hesitancy, but she was thinking of the flustered face she'd seen earlier. If that woman was the Reverend Pascoe, she had her own troubles, troubles Audrey didn't want to get mixed up in.

'Oh, she's the soul of charity, Lamorna,' she insisted. 'And she has more beds than she needs in that old place. Whereas the pub's nearly full, what with Trevor and Griffin both living at home again.'

Griffin. The taxi driver. He told me to come and eat at the pub where he lives, she thought, and then, just as quickly, wondered why she cared. 'It's a family business then?'

'They all are, round about. The Kingcups, now, they've run the pub here going back centuries.'

'What about your family? You're from the village too, right?' She wasn't terribly interested. But Morgan's conversation drowned out the silence from the back seat. The policeman seemed to take it kindly, smiling and launching into his life story.

'My family had a farm a step further inland, generations of us. I made myself a bit of a black sheep going off to join the police. Apples don't tend to fall far from the tree here, generally. I worked up in London once myself – been posted all over. Now they've put me back here, close to the old place, and I'm glad. I spent so much time moving about, focused on the job, I never got a chance to build much of what you'd call a personal life. Nice to be among familiar faces once more. Comes a time you want to share things. You'll find that out for yourselves one day.'

Audrey refrained from turning around to look at Noah. He was evidently still brooding, because he said nothing to ease her discomfort. 'Nobody waiting for you here then? Old flame?' She was eager to move off the topic of her own romance, but she felt a bit sorry for the policeman. He'd sounded wistful. And look at him, all geniality and rumpled clothes. He deserved someone who'd sort out his missing shirt buttons.

'It's a small pond, not full of fish. Mind you, Stella Penrose was really something when we were growing up. I met her in school, the kids from this village and a few others, plus the farms round about, we all fed into the same secondary. She was the best-looking girl this side of the Helford.'

He lapsed into silence again, another sad silence, though not on his own behalf this time. Audrey was picturing the woman on the ground, bloodied by her own hand. She imagined he was, too. After a minute he shook himself and carried on.

'I'm glad she made something of her life, even if... You'd never have guessed it, staying in that house, but Stella came from nothing. The Penroses were a bad lot.'

'What kind of bad lot?'

'Oh, usual sort – drunks, ne'er-do-wells. Smugglers, in the old days. Now Stella, she was always ambitious. You knew right from the start she'd be going places. She had her troubles, but she made it up the hill in the end.'

Audrey wanted to ask what sort of troubles, but she decided it wasn't her business. Given the suspicion surrounding Stella's death, the less she was embroiled in her life the better. She wondered if Noah was listening in the back; he'd certainly seemed curious enough about Stella when she was alive. But he was unreadable, cocooned in bad feelings and the noise of the road, staring out the window at the running rain.

Morgan cleared his throat and said, 'I am sorry you two will have to stick around. I'm sure you have full lives to get back to in town. But at least you'll get to see in Golowan.'

'Stella was telling us about it,' she replied. 'Sounds like quite the tradition.'

'She tell you it was all about dragons?' He smiled indulgently. 'She had an eye for a picturesque detail, did Stella. Nowadays it's just a community thing, a chance for the village to get together. Course its feet still stand in the old ways, let's say.'

'Old ways?' Audrey felt very little curiosity about the midsummer rites of a village she hadn't heard about till today and wished she could start forgetting tomorrow. But as long as Morgan kept talking it kept her mind from circling endlessly around the dead body, the dark night, the snake watching in the corner of the room.

'Well, all that snake stuff, for instance.' Audrey's neck prickled; why had he chosen to talk about snakes at the exact moment she'd been thinking of the sculpture? But he carried on in a reassuringly dry vein. 'Some think that came all the way from the Phoenicians, even before the rise of the Celts. You see, the real draw of this place is tin. And it was tin that drew people from far and – ah.'

Audrey's heart sank as the tin talk made a reappearance, but she was spared the finer points. They were pulling up in front of the vicarage.

She could see the church crouched over it, a shadow blacker than the sky, and dripping yews clustered all along the walk. The woman from the cemetery, who must be Lamorna

Pascoe, was waiting at the open door under a fanlight. She had on a pink towelling bathrobe; Audrey felt a bit funny seeing her throat naked of its vocational mark. She'd come out further from the door than she needed to, and the rain was plastering her thin pale hair to the sides of her round cheeks.

'Couple of strays for you,' called out DI Morgan. He was carrying Audrey's bag; once again, Noah hadn't offered.

'What an awful thing,' said Reverend Pascoe, backing through the doorway and trying to take a bag at the same time, blocking everyone's way and making their entry to the house more difficult with her attempts to help. 'You poor, poor dears.'

'It's Stella who needs sympathy,' said Noah, with surprising vehemence.

'Yes, of course,' said the vicar, after a pause. 'Come through, let me show you your room. You must be exhausted.'

Audrey certainly was. It occurred to her now, as the adrenaline ebbed from her system, that this was the second time in twelve hours she was being shown to a strange room after an exhausting journey. Even before everything had happened, she'd been tired from the heat, the travel and the depressing influence of her disappointment; then had come the added exhausting effects of an argument and too many glasses of wine; and finally the awful tension of seeing a dead woman, and explaining herself to the police. She could barely muster the energy to say goodbye to DI Morgan as he was leaving, and to acknowledge his reminder that he'd need to question them again. It was nearly four in the morning. She wanted nothing more than to sleep.

Almost nothing, anyway. When the vicar showed them to one room, obviously assuming they'd sleep there together, she found the energy to object. 'I'm afraid you've got the wrong end of the stick,' she said. 'Noah and I won't be sharing.'

'Oh.' The woman's face went as pink as her robe, and she tried to brush away some of the thin locks of wet hair sticking to it. 'I'm terribly sorry. There is another room, but I haven't put out sheets—'

'Two unmarried people can't share a bed under the vicarage roof.' This was an absurd reason, but she hoped Lamorna would get the hint.

'You needn't worry about that! We might still celebrate ancient rituals down here, but we do know we live in the twenty-first century,' she said with a little laugh.

'Come on, Audrey,' said Noah. 'Don't be like this.' At least her pettiness had needled him out of his stupor.

She didn't back down. 'Give me the sheets and I'll do it myself.' Noah gave her a look of betrayal and shut himself in the room.

Reverend Pascoe came back with a pile of faded flowery bedding, and smiled nervously. 'I do apologise – only everyone said it was a couple coming to stay in the big house.'

'It was,' said Audrey, and then turned into her own room and shut the door firmly behind her before there could be any questions. It wasn't fair to make this vicar, who'd done nothing but give them a place to stay for the night, feel uncomfortable. But it was driving her mad, the feeling that everyone in the village was talking about them, that she was an object of curiosity and speculation. To have to break up

(But are we breaking up? she thought) under the gaze of friends would have been bad enough; curious strangers, and a suicide, made it unbearable.

She was too tired to make the bed up properly, though. She put on the fitted sheet and then simply pulled the naked duvet over herself. As she switched off the light, she noticed that the picture over the bed wasn't one of Jesus, as she would have expected – instead it was a scene from Eden, Adam and Eve naked, eyeing each other, hands all over those apples. And writhing between Eve's breasts, coiling around her neck, forking its tongue into her ear: a snake.

Audrey was sure she would fall asleep as soon as her eyes were closed, but the moment she did, she saw Stella, lying there, her yellow pyjamas twisted up and the silk stained red. Her hand clawed around the knife.

Suddenly Audrey couldn't breathe. She was sure she wasn't alone in the room. The scraping branches of the woods at Trevennick House; the hand on the knife; something, something was there. Something slithering and writhing, its long form strange. And it wanted her.

The terror was bad. As bad as when she was a child. She'd thought she'd escaped all that when she left home, but now here she was again, heart stopped, lungs empty, shooting pains in her chest. Her limbs were frozen, and she couldn't think how to make it stop, the only thought going around and around: *Something's here, something's here.*

Audrey didn't know how long it was before her hands unlocked. She clawed at the cord of the bedside lamp and then, when it came on, found herself unable to open her tightly shut eyes and look around the room, because *it's still here, it's still here*. She drew a few shuddering breaths and then made herself look.

There was nothing lurking, only a chintz armchair and a case of old books. Slowly her heartbeat grew regular, and the panic attack subsided. But she was too frightened to turn out the light again. She lay staring at the strange room until dawn greyed the edges of the curtain, and then subsided into anxious sleep.

ST JOHN'S EVE

CHAPTER 8

Audrey woke to strong sunshine, and realised she'd slept late. It was hot again – the storm had broken without refreshing the air. She felt flushed and sticky. Escaping duvet feathers were pricking her skin.

Out of the window were great sky-reflecting stretches of water in the garden and the lane and fields beyond, as well as some damage: freshly downed tree limbs, trunks showing bright and wet where branches had been torn away. Along the lane branches were moving. She thought it must be a clean-up effort, but then, as they neared and resolved, she realised it was another obby oss, being carried towards the green.

She turned away from the window feeling a vague distaste and considered the room she had washed up in. It seemed far less threatening this morning – not creepy, just faded. Old furniture, massive and dark; flower patterns on everything: the chair, the sheets, the curtains, a similar pattern on the wallpaper. There was that framed print, with its strangling snake, which, she could see now, was an engraving of Cranach or Dürer, too crudely made to be identifiable. The snake looked spindly in daylight, not powerful at all, and Eve was cross-eyed.

At the bookcase, she tipped a few volumes this way and that, green and brown bindings that might have been fifty years old or a hundred. *The Veil of Isis. The Golden Bough.* Books on myth and magic. All a bit occult for a vicarage, but she supposed priests must be interested in the sacred in general.

Fearful of running into Noah in the hall, she explored quietly until she found a bathroom. The taps had made a dark rust mark on the tub, and everything was covered in limescale and the kind of greasy scum that builds up in rarely cleaned toilets and kitchens; but the water was hot, and she stood under it for a long time, hoping yesterday would wash off. Stella's twisted dead form: down the drain. The Noah situation: down the drain. The darkness lurking between the trees everywhere: down the drain. When she started imagining work emails swirling down there too, and the broken blind waiting to be fixed back at her flat, she decided she was probably ready to get out.

Downstairs she found more furniture that had probably been here since Victoria was queen, more dusty bookshelves, more chintz, everything a little shabby and neglected, as though the vicar spent all her time elsewhere. Still no crucifix, which Audrey thought was odd, but then, when was the last time she'd visited a vicarage?

The kitchen, though it was empty, did seem inhabited, the air still lively with the passage of a human presence. There was bread on the side, and butter and jam jars in a gossipy knot on the round table. She made herself some toast, and was spooning out some marmalade when she heard a shot and froze.

Probably fireworks, she told herself. At least, that's what it would be in London. Then the sound came again – crack! – and she was sure it must be a gunshot. She waited, heart thumping. A wasp circled the jam, but she couldn't wave it away.

Then Lamorna Pascoe came in through the kitchen door, looking hot but correct in her restored collar and black. 'Oh, good, you're up. I worried the shot would wake you. The crows get at my raspberries, and I can't have it. Got one, I'm pleased to say.' She leaned a rifle against the wall. The vicar's eyes were a little glazed and her cheeks flushed, as they had been last night, and, indeed, the first time Audrey saw her. Now, though, she looked excited, not embarrassed. Audrey tried to hurry through her breakfast as Reverend Pascoe bustled about making herself tea. But the vicar seemed to want a chat. A vocational requirement, Audrey supposed. 'It'll be a strange festival, this year, after the death,' Lamorna said.

'She seems to have been quite a presence in the village.'

'People in the big house loom large over the rest of us.'

Audrey wasn't sure how to respond – the vicar's tone was less mournful and more observational than she would have expected. But then, she hadn't liked Stella, and she'd had much less time to form an opinion than this woman had. She doubted the dead woman made regular appearances in church. Still she was surprised when the vicar continued, 'No sin goes unpunished.'

'Sin? Do you mean suicide?'

'Oh no. I meant vanity,' replied Lamorna without hesitation. 'That was her sin. That woman thought she was owed everything in this life.'

Audrey blinked. It might be a priestly remark, but it wasn't very Christian. She tried to steer the conversation into safer territory. 'Well, I hope it doesn't ruin the celebrations. I hear they're quite something.'

'If anything, emotion may run higher, no bad thing for Golowan. The river takes her cut, after all. But what about you? I can't imagine this is how you pictured your trip.'

'We just wanted a long weekend away. Noah…' But then she remembered his pleading looks last night, his desire not to be named as the architect of this trip or have any of his deeper motivations, which she still hadn't understood, exposed. She wasn't sure she owed him that discretion; and yet her own instinct to extricate herself from the situation as quickly and with as few complications as possible was served by keeping the story simple. And, as far as she knew, it was perfectly simple. 'He seemed to think I'd like this bit of the country.'

'Don't you?'

'I'm more of a city person.'

'You aren't glued to your phone like some.'

Again, Audrey was struck by the slightly intrusive nature of the comment. It wasn't hostile exactly, but Reverend Pascoe seemed unable to speak without stepping a little over the line. She wasn't the person Audrey was going to open up to about her reasons for disliking small villages and dark nights. 'No,

I'm not particularly busy or important. But I like to feel the buzz, you know.'

The other woman nodded thoughtfully. She began unloading the dishwasher, mostly full, Audrey saw, of mugs and teaspoons. It seemed the Reverend Pascoe lived alone, though Audrey had already guessed that from the way DI Morgan had spoken of her. As she stowed the crockery, she began to explain Audrey to herself.

'People often feel uncomfortable with the peace out here. I don't say quiet, mind you – the countryside's just as noisy as the city, between the farmers and the birds. But there's a certain kind of calm that descends when you're close to nature. A space that's made. And often people find that something in them they weren't prepared to meet comes out, once there's room for it.'

'I wouldn't say it's been calm since I got here.'

'Oh dear, no, you're quite right!' Lamorna Pascoe began to giggle. This woman's all over the place, thought Audrey. How does she get through the service? 'I'm afraid I was on pastoral autopilot there. When you're a vicar, it's a bit like offering biscuits – whether you're thinking about it or not, out pops the tin, and with it a nice warm cup of spiritual guidance.'

'Vocational incontinence, you might say.'

The giggle stopped, and the other woman looked narrowly at Audrey, who ducked behind her mug and tried to look innocent. 'You might.' Then she brightened: 'Still, Golowan is a good time to have an encounter with Mother Nature. And all her helpers. Have a wander round, you might have an interesting encounter with yourself.'

I've had enough interesting encounters in the past twenty-four hours, thank you, thought Audrey, but aloud she agreed that walking around was a good idea, as she was stuck here for the present.

'Just make sure you're down by the river by dusk,' said the vicar. 'You wouldn't want to miss the ceremony.'

'What's involved?'

'Ah. It's hard to explain to an outsider. You've got to experience it.' The other woman closed her eyes and breathed deeply, as though sinking into powerful memories. 'The real purpose is to restore our balance with nature. In modern life, we can be in the habit of taking more than we give. Golowan is when we give. Water always finds a way, and the river will have her share. So it's better we give than she takes.'

Audrey nodded, though this made little sense to her, and stood. 'Time for that encounter with myself.'

When she looked back, Lamorna Pascoe was still standing in the kitchen doorway, watching her go.

Exiting through the garden, she saw one of the crows the vicar had shot, pinned against the hedge with its wings out as a warning to the rest. Audrey shuddered, wondering how that restored nature's balance, and turned towards the river. She hoped she wouldn't run into anyone carrying an obby oss that looked like a bird. It would seem too sinister in the light of her hostess's rough horticultural justice.

Unsure how to fill the time, she wandered around the village for a while. She kept checking her phone, in case the police had called with more questions, but the reception, when it appeared, disappeared seconds later. They would just have to find her if they wanted her. Without phone service there was also no chance of catching up on emails, which was a relief – she was sure she would have five messages from Jemima at the publisher's, all asking about her overdue work, each using more kisses than the last as her panic mounted and the revised deadline approached. Nor, without her phone, could she call and tell anyone what had happened. But who would she tell? Her friends, such as they were, didn't get this kind of insight into her life. She might have talked to Noah about it if he weren't the heart of the problem. But he was. So she walked, going up and down the few narrow streets, glancing discreetly into cottage windows and nodding awkwardly at villagers, who looked at her with frank curiosity.

What would she be doing if she were still with Noah? She thought of the elaborate and ultimately useless itinerary she had prepared for Paris: spreadsheets of recommended restaurants, unmissable museum collections, buildings of architectural note. Had Noah thought to create anything like that for down here? Had he planned for her pleasure? Or had it been an empty exercise from the beginning, designed around whatever mysterious private end he'd refused to make clear? She'd probably never know now what he'd been thinking. She was disappointed in him. And in herself. There had been those little gaps from the start, like a skip in a record. But she'd ignored that stutter and catch in the relationship for the best part of a year. He was good-looking; she'd thought he might help her career. But was that all? Was she that shallow? There was something between them, she insisted to herself, otherwise she wouldn't feel upset about it probably ending.

The pub didn't open till noon, and it seemed to be the only place to get lunch. No cafe, only a combined shop and post office, also closed, and with windows so dusty she wondered when it had last been open. She could see why Stella had wanted to shake things up. At the green a few villagers were conferring over the preparation of a bonfire. She tried to ignore their stares as she crossed the grass. Wherever you went in this village, you were watched.

She found a bench by the river, and took a seat with her back turned firmly to the watchers. Here and there the banks were embroidered with flowers, but they'd reached that point in the summer when most of the blossoms were gone and everything was covered in encroaching green. The leaves massed into darkness between the trees on the opposite bank, even in the glare of late morning.

At a loose end, she turned to the thing that had always kept unwelcome thoughts at bay: drawing. She felt better as soon as she had extracted her sketchbook from her bag. Looking away from the shadows at the sunnier part of the prospect – the descending green, the flower-trimmed river, the clustering cottages on either side of the sweetly arching bridge – she thought it would make a good preparatory sketch for the next book. She really must get down to drafting some images if she wasn't going to miss another deadline.

She filled the first page or two with studies she could use: twee village scenes, the perfect backdrop for a winsomely endangered hedgehog. As her quick strokes quietened her mind, though, other images began to emerge. Cottages and wildflowers gave way to Stella Penrose twisting this way and that across the page, her pyjamas soaked in blood, her hand on the knife she'd used to stab herself.

A cloud passing over the sun cooled Audrey momentarily, and she shook herself out of the world of her drawings and back into the real. She shuddered looking at the pictures she'd made, but she'd also relieved the pressure inside her skull. She'd been so blocked lately, and now she was filling the pages of her sketchbook faster than she had in months.

It had always been like this: when something bad happened, she had to turn it into pencil line or charcoal shading before she could let it go. There was a folder in her studio full of drawings of the airing cupboard, the one in her childhood home. They were almost pure black. She knew she shouldn't return there. But she kept coming back. As though some part of her were still trapped there, lost in the dark.

CHAPTER 9

The sun had at last glared its way to noon. Audrey went in search of lunch. The pub was cave-like, its dim cool depths a welcome shelter from the hot, thick air outside, and her eyes took a moment to adjust. Trailing plants grew over many of the windows, greening the light within. The chairs were down off the tables, and she could see sauce bottles and cutlery laid, but there was no one behind the bar. Then a black woman in late middle age emerged from the kitchen, glass and polishing cloth in hand. There was the Kingcup face again, the one Audrey had seen already on Griffin and Trevor; this must be their mother.

She was calmer than both her sons – less glintingly cocky than the one, less brooding than the other. She looked at Audrey evenly, continuing to polish the glass, and only asked what she wanted by raising her eyebrows.

Audrey felt exposed, somehow, in that quiet, knowing gaze, and giggled foolishly as she ordered. 'I'm so thirsty in this heat! A shandy, maybe?' As soon as she said it, she felt silly. She never drank shandy. Not since she was a child and her mother had let her have a sip at Sunday lunch.

The woman nodded and pulled the drink, lemonade and then beer. 'Your friend's thirsty in the heat too,' she said as she handed Audrey her drink and nodded to the other side of the bar. Audrey, peering round, saw Noah slumped in a leather armchair. She froze and considered leaving, but he'd heard the exchange and looked up, seeing her.

'Hey.' He half-started out of his chair. 'Join me. Please.'

Audrey sat, moving with defensive precision, placing her glass on the low table before them, brushing something off her jeans. She took a moment trying to decide what to say, looking around at the room, the pictures on the walls. They were sat by the fireplace, unlit in this weather but clearly much used at other seasons. The mantel held pewter mugs, as it probably had for a few hundred years. Above it was a print like the one she'd seen in Stella's house, men from another century smashing tankards above a barrel. Eventually, when she'd made him wait a while, she looked back at Noah. 'You must have got here just before me.'

'Doesn't seem to be anywhere else to go,' he said. He took a sip of his drink. Whisky, it looked like.

'Bit early, isn't it?' She didn't really blame him. After yesterday, she felt the need of a lunchtime drink, too. But she found that she was still angry with him, and being prim was one way to mark the distance between them.

He shrugged and gulped the rest of it back. 'Last night—'

'Yes.' She sipped her own drink, fizzy, sweet-bitter and cool. 'I dreamed about it. Or rather, I kept seeing it. I couldn't fall asleep.'

'Creepy house, eh?'

'I'm pretty sure someone died of consumption in my bed in 1845.'

He smiled. 'Or tin miner's lung? Is that a thing?'

'I'm sure DI Morgan could tell you all about it.'

That got an actual chuckle. In spite of her intention to be frosty, everything suddenly felt easy between them. Where the hell did they stand? When he looked at her a certain way, when his smile fell on her, it felt like the relationship she'd begun to take for granted was still there, like they could slip back into it.

The heat had made even the weak shandy go straight to her head, and, loosened by laughter and the mild drink, she said, 'I'm sorry to put it this way, given the show you're about to hang, but – are we just good on paper?'

Noah gave the pun a laughing wince and then turned serious. 'I'm sorry things are turning out this way. It's not what I was hoping for.'

'What were you hoping for?'

He mulled this over, and when he opened his mouth she thought a real answer would come out, but instead he said, 'You want to get some lunch?'

Audrey sighed. She'd hoped that, by the end of this conversation, they'd be definitively together or apart. But she was hungry too, and reasoned that everything's harder on an empty stomach, so she replied, 'Sure, anything. Fish and chips, I guess.'

She watched him as he paid for their lunch, smiling at the woman behind the bar, making the most of his charming face. Being the person she could slip back into something with. But she knew that when he turned he would vanish into himself, somewhere she wasn't invited to follow. Like he had on the train. Like he had from the very beginning.

Noah came back over, his smile fading. In a way, she was glad he wasn't keeping up the pretence with her. Even if he wasn't being perfectly honest. Neither was she. Audrey decided to be merciful, and while they waited for the food she made small talk, or what passed for small talk in their situation. She asked if the police had contacted him again, and he said yes, DI Morgan had told him to wait here, and to tell her to wait too. So. They'd be there for a while. They lapsed into a silence which was heavy but not uneasy, each taking slow sips. When the food arrived, they ate it avidly, trading sauce bottles and remarking on how hungry they were. Finally, she sat back and looked at him squarely and repeated her earlier question: 'So what were you hoping for?'

She was sure he would withdraw, the pattern demanded it, but he didn't. His smile faded and his already dark eyes darkened further. 'It isn't easy, letting people in.'

'Is that why we came here? You were trying to let me in? Into what?'

'I guess we were supposed to know each other better. I think we both have areas of our lives we've left... fenced off. Don't you?'

This was so unexpected, she almost spit her shandy back into the glass. It was her role to push for more intimate disclosures; her own lack of openness was so much easier to hide when she could criticise him. Well, he had called her bluff. For the second time. 'I do.'

'One of us has to open up first, I guess.'

'We wouldn't be here if it weren't for you.' She gestured at the pub, the village outside, the whole situation. 'So, I think it's your job to start. What would you have told me about, if this trip had gone according to plan?'

'I wanted to tell you about—'

'Oi! We need to talk!'

Audrey turned, startled at the angry shout. It came from the man standing behind her. He was squared up as though prepared for a fight, and his neck was flushed. His sun-bleached hair and shorts, together with the stone hanging from a strip of leather around his neck, suggested that he was a surfer. But apparently not with a surfer's laid-back attitude.

'I'm sorry, I don't know you.' Noah was back behind his facade, frowning and supercilious, all the gatekeeping superiority he used at the gallery on display.

'Yeah, but I know *you*. You're the people who were staying with my Stella.'

So this must be Cameron, assistant and fiancé. Audrey looked to Noah, and saw that the realisation had quickly taken the wind out of his sails. Gone was the incipient smirk and flared nostrils of the urbane sophisticate rebuffing an uncouth intruder. Now he looked forlorn. He seemed unable to reply, so Audrey, annoyed as she was at the timing of the interruption, took it upon herself to speak. 'I'm so sorry for your loss.'

'No you're not. You had something to do with it.'

Now Audrey was the one flushing angrily. As best she could while sitting in a deep leather armchair, she squared up to him. 'Of course not. We were horrified by what happened.

You're not usually signing up to witness a suicide when you rent an Airbnb.'

She had tipped over the line between firm and tactless, and she cringed as she played back the words in her head. But Cameron wasn't about to be placated anyway. He pointed an accusing finger. 'All I know is, I go off for my stag. Everything's fine. When I come back she's... she's...' Here emotion overcame him, and he stood there, finger still raised, chest heaving with rageful grief, or grieving rage.

'Do you have any idea why she'd have done it?'

Noah's question seemed to disarm him, and he slumped in one of the chairs next to them.

Audrey inspected Cameron, finding room for curiosity now he was less confrontational. She wondered about the age difference between him and Stella, and how they'd come to fall in love. But that was old-fashioned, she chided herself; and anyway she'd seen first-hand the kind of attention Stella could turn on a younger man.

'No fucking clue. She wasn't that type of woman. She was so full of life force, she really embodied the eternal feminine, you know? Did she tell you about our rewilding project?' He looked up hopefully, evidently wanting to hear that she'd spoken of it on her last night alive.

'I'm sorry,' said Noah, 'we didn't talk about that.'

'Oh.' Cameron's lower lip hung down sulkily. Then he pointed at their empty plates. 'You're aware that fully 80% of the world's fisheries are overexploited, right?'

Audrey and Noah shared a look. This hardly seemed relevant, but it was probably best to indulge the bereaved fiancé.

'So what did you talk about?' Cameron asked.

'Um, history really. Local history,' Noah said. 'She seemed to think a lot of changes were necessary to revive the place. Maybe she meant your rewilding project.' He looked expectantly at Cameron.

'It's how we met. She'd come back to Cornwall, bought the place and wanted to return it to its natural state. I was working for a tree-planting initiative, she got my name and hired me to help her. Other than the woods by the river, it's mostly farmland up there, eaten down to bare grass by cows and sheep. Globally, we have less than a century's worth of topsoil left.' He looked down at his dangling hands, mournful. Audrey couldn't tell if he was grieving for Stella or the depleted soil.

'It sounds a very worthwhile project.'

'It's what I've always wanted to do. But we were going to do it together.' He covered his face with his hands and his shoulders shook a little.

'I'm sure you'll be able to carry on the work,' said Audrey, though she realised it was a hollow promise. Who knew if Cameron would inherit the land? They hadn't made it to the wedding.

'It won't be the same,' came his broken reply. 'She was so passionate about it, too. Together we were going to claim the wave.'

'She was an incredible woman.' Noah reached out a hand and laid it on Cameron's shoulder.

'If only she hadn't…' The rest was lost in sobs. Noah circled his hand on the man's back. Audrey's eyes met his, and she felt a softness towards him.

Cameron was wiping his face now, a little sheepish. He looked around, as though to see who'd caught him crying, and let out a tsk of annoyance when he spotted Griffin and Trevor Kingcup at the bar. Griffin was leaning on an elbow, watching them, and his dog was also staring. For some reason, Audrey blushed.

'Look, sorry about what I said. I just feel…' Cameron blew out his cheeks, searching for the word. It didn't come. 'I should go. I'll see you around.' He stood up and left, ignoring Noah's efforts to retain him.

'You were very sweet with him,' Audrey said once he was gone.

Noah shrugged off the compliment. 'Easy enough to be sympathetic to someone in his position.'

'Is it though? I've never known the right thing to say after a death. You saw me, I kept putting my foot in it.'

'Yeah, well, he didn't make the softest entry. Poor guy. You'd be looking for someone to blame too, I suppose.'

'But I don't know that I'd pick on the least likely candidates.'

Noah made a doubtful moue. 'I'm not sure we're the least likely. We were in the house when it happened, after all.'

'And you, at any rate, were awake.' She wouldn't have dared this challenge when she first sat down. But the tension between them had eased so much – between the drink and their shared confrontation of the bereaved Cameron, she felt like they were getting along as well as they ever had. Maybe they shouldn't break up after all.

'But I didn't do anything. Surely you believe me?'

'I do, of course, but you just admitted you've been holding things back. Why have you been so weird since we came down here? What were you talking about with Stella after I went to bed?'

'I'll admit the conversation got a little... intense. But it certainly wasn't for the reason you thought last night.'

'There was nothing between you two?'

'Obviously nothing like that! The truth is... The truth is... Okay, the truth is that I'd wanted to meet Stella because—'

Then, with Noah finally about to be straightforward with her, they were interrupted again. This time the intruder was friendly, but he was no more welcome for that.

'How are you two finding the village?' asked Griffin, approaching with a wide smile and a pint of beer. The dog followed close behind. Griffin installed himself in the third armchair with a sigh, ignoring Audrey's small gesture of protest. She breathed heavily through her nose in frustration, and his smile grew broader.

Noah looked back and forth between them and then stood. 'I need some air.'

'I'll come with you,' said Audrey, rising to join him. 'We really need to finish our talk.'

'No, stay. Someone needs to be here in case DI Morgan comes along. And I need to clear my head. Five minutes, I promise, and then we can talk all you want.'

And he was gone.

CHAPTER 10

'Thanks very much for interrupting.'

'You're welcome, Aud.'

'We're not on nickname terms.'

'But Aud suits you.' He sipped his beer and smacked satisfied lips, then, seeing the irritation on Audrey's face, dropped a bit of the effrontery and continued, 'I'm sorry, you're only as odd as anyone else.'

She rolled her eyes. 'Incredibly graceful apology accepted. Look, I was in the middle of something with Noah. Could you just… go away?' The upside of his cockiness, she supposed, was that she could tell him exactly what she thought without feeling rude. Now he leaned closer, and surprised her by sounding genuinely apologetic.

'Well, I did say that I thought you two would want to be left alone, after everything that's happened. But I was under Mum's orders, and you don't question those.'

'Why would your mother care whether two strangers carry on a private conversation in her pub?' She turned to look at the woman behind the bar, and turned immediately back when she found her staring in their direction, smiling slightly and polishing yet another glass.

'She said your man needed to talk to Cameron.'

'He's not my man. We're breaking up. Probably.'

'Oh. Right.' For once, Griffin looked wrong-footed. 'Well, either way, when Mum says two people need to talk, they need to talk. She's got a sense about these things.'

'You're trying to tell me she's clairvoyant?'

'She probably wouldn't call it that. Would you, Mum?' he shouted over his shoulder.

'What?'

'Call yourself clairvoyant?'

At the bar, his mother snorted. 'You spend as long a time working in a pub as I have and you come to know a thing or two about human nature,' she called over.

'You've been here long?' asked Audrey.

'One whole life long. I grew up in this pub. Just like these boys.' She gestured at Griffin, and at Trevor waiting at the other end of the bar, then moved off to talk to her other son.

Griffin smiled at Audrey. 'She's not listening, don't worry.'

'Privacy would be convenient, if we had anything we needed to say to each other.'

'Just because there's nothing we need to say doesn't mean there's nothing we *want* to say.'

It was infuriating, the way he met every attempt to put him in his place with a grin or a riposte. Like a roly-poly toy, bouncing back no matter how hard you pushed. She ought to go and find Noah, find out what he wanted to tell her;

but it seemed important to stay and put Griffin Kingcup in his place. As soon as she could think of a comeback. 'So, ah, you grew up in the pub?' she asked, temporarily at a loss for a more cutting remark.

'Was in my gran's family, the Kingcups. Mum's dad was in the merchant navy, sailing out of the West Indies. He met Gran on shore leave while she was on a day out along the coast. Mum didn't meet him till she was twenty. But then my dad disappeared too. Mum has a saying: men make terrible fathers.'

Audrey thought of her own father. Her childhood in the house where the clocks ticked so loudly, signalling another second you hadn't set him off – or one second closer to the next time you did.

'I'd tend to agree with her.'

'I'm sorry to hear it.' And he did sound it. It was strange; this was the second time she'd met Griffin, and they'd already shared nearly as much about their childhoods as she and Noah had told each other in ten months.

'Well, seems like you turned out all right. I mean, fairly irritating, but fine.'

'Why thank you.' Griffin grinned, but then looked at his mother and brother, speaking in low tones over the bar, and the grin faded. 'I did all right, but it was tougher on Trev. He was that bit older. Plus, you know, we stand out a bit, living down here. He always had to protect me in school. Had to toughen up. Whereas yours truly remains as feckless and charming as the day he was born.'

'Debatable.'

'No, honestly, I am. Look, talk to my brother, you'll see. Compared to him I'm a total smoothie. Oi, Trev!' He waved the other man over. 'Don't be upset if he growls.'

Trevor didn't growl, but he did seem more interested in the dog than in meeting Audrey. He sat and murmured to it, stroking its pale yellow fur and only occasionally glancing up at her. 'Good boy. We got rid of that Cameron together, didn't we?'

'And why do you care about getting rid of him?' Audrey was struck by the phrase. It seemed tactless, or maybe reckless, to use it so soon after a death.

Trevor looked her full in the face for the first time and said, 'They're going to kill the river, him and her. They were, I should say.'

'What do you mean? He just told me that they were rewilding her land, surely that's good for the river?'

Trevor snorted and turned back to the dog. Griffin watched him. He seemed a bit quieter around his brother, anxiously attentive. She'd noticed it in the taxi yesterday too. But Trevor had been quarrelling with Reverend Pascoe then. And arguing with a vicar is cause for concern, no matter how strange she might be. Audrey wondered what that tense exchange had been about.

'Trevor works on the river,' volunteered Griffin, after the silence had extended for a while.

'Nobody knows her like I do,' said his brother, repetitively stroking the dog without looking up.

'Knows who?' Audrey asked.

'The river.' He looked at her like she was slow, like

everybody talked about bodies of water as if they were women. 'I've had mussel ropes on the estuary since I was eighteen. I've gone up every tributary, every last creek in my boat. I know her.'

'I'm sure you do,' said Audrey. Trevor's vehemence was notable, and she felt obliged to placate him. He was a little frightening – everything open, sunny, and glinting with mischief in Griffin was twisted inwards with intensity in his brother.

'And I know what it would do to her if that woman built those houses. Mind you, we need houses. But we need the river more.'

'Wait, what houses? That's not what I heard she was doing with her land.'

'Can you trust what she says?'

'Look, maybe you didn't like her, but you shouldn't speak ill of the dead.' Audrey was a little surprised at her own directness, but there was something about the way people acted down here that encouraged her to cut to the chase. Less song and dance was required than in city life.

'Just passing over doesn't make somebody trustworthy.'

'Trev—' But Griffin's attempt to halt his brother's flow was unsuccessful.

'It's true what they say. The river takes its cut. Our family has suffered—'

'Trevor Kingcup.' This attempt was successful, but it didn't come from Griffin. Their mother had spoken softly, with none of the urgency of either of her sons, and yet her voice had cut across theirs with utter finality.

Trevor looked at her, glaring and working his jaw a little, and then turned and left the pub, roiling anger darkening the atmosphere in his wake.

'Griffin, I think you should go get another keg from downstairs. We don't want the taps running dry on Golowan.'

'She means she wants to talk to you,' he said in an undertone as he stood and went to do his mother's bidding.

'I say what I mean, young man, I don't need you to translate for me. You get that keg and then go see if they need help on the green.' But her tone was indulgent, and she smiled at her son as he leaned across the bar to plant a kiss on her cheek. Then she turned her penetrating gaze back to Audrey. 'Now, young miss down from London, my name is Morwenna. I'd like to know more about you. Come sit here and tell me.'

The most surprising thing about all of this was that after a lifetime of not telling people about herself, that's exactly what Audrey did.

Audrey had grown up in a little house in a little village nestled into the Cotswold hills, far enough from London to still be a place in its own right rather than a commuter haven. Honeysuckle grew over her door; most buildings she knew were made of golden stone. She'd been in the Girl Guides as a child, and delighted in finding fallen birds' nests and mastering complex knots.

But her home hadn't been as idyllic as the setting. All her memories up until a certain age were suffused with a milky, summery, sweet-scented atmosphere. Then everything soured.

She was six or seven when the sweetness went out of the cuckoo's call. A back injury put her father out of work. Her mother got a job in the nearest town to make up the lost money. She was always driving away for a shift, or coming home tired. Things like cooking and cleaning didn't get done, or not well. Audrey's father wasn't the kind of man to take over domestic duties from his wife, or to respond to his adverse circumstances with grace. He didn't go looking for a good life he could lead in his new condition.

Instead, he seethed quietly at the unfairness of it all. He lay on the sofa nursing his injury with carefully placed pillows and beer; eventually beer wasn't strong enough. He snapped at his daughter when she made noise in the room, when she tried to show him things she'd found in the garden, when she spilled something in the kitchen trying to make a snack. Eventually he did more than snap.

A favourite technique was to lock her in the pitch-black cupboard at the top of the stairs. He'd leave her in there for hours, until her mother returned from work and, saying nothing, let her out. Audrey always wondered where the back pain went as he dragged her shouting to her prison, shoved her in and turned the lock. He seemed well enough then.

The neighbours must have known things weren't right. Terraced houses have thin walls. The garden overgrew, brambles clawed the fences on either side, and inside Audrey cried for mercy. But they said nothing; too difficult, in a village, where everyone knows each other, and a disagreement can make trips to the post office awkward for years. Sometimes she pleaded with her mother to do something, to leave, and her mother looked tired, and terribly sad, and pleaded back, *But what would people think?* At primary school, her teacher was bored and close to retiring, and took Audrey's class through the rudiments of learning with a dull, dutiful air. She didn't ask pupils questions about their lives, or act on information they volunteered in their desperation. She didn't take any notice of the clawed monsters and seeping shadows that Audrey couldn't stop drawing.

By the time Audrey was at secondary school, she'd learned to hate the mixture of claustrophobia and isolation that she now associated with village life. She was also terrified of the dark. The dark of the cupboard. The dark of the empty road outside their house. The dark of country nights, and the sinister somethings that had crept out into them from her unhappy home. She was determined to escape to a better, brighter life. Her worn-out mother and bitter father insisted she do 'something practical', which didn't mean art college, so she chose graphic design as the next best thing. Why she ceded to their wishes she wasn't sure, because after taking the money to get to university, she had taken nothing else from them. She got a job as soon as she arrived, and never returned home. Her mother called occasionally, and she gave her minimal answers, letting her know that yes, she was alive, yes, she'd found work, yes, thank you, the extinct animals book was doing well. Behind the weary voice she could sense her father like some dark beast, lying on the sofa, his eyes red with booze, his breath just above a growl.

That was the world she'd left behind. Art had been her route out, and her link to sanity before she escaped. She drew the horrible things she saw in the dark; she drew what she wanted. Nobody could tell her not to. She moved to London, but though the street lights and the human bustle comforted her, she wasn't happy. She'd never broken into Noah's world, nor had she built one of her own; most of her friends were more like acquaintances. She kept waiting to arrive in a different life, and felt the taint of the bad old one clinging to her. Her body might have escaped, but her mind was still stuck.

Why she was moved to tell Morwenna Kingcup all this, she didn't understand, and by the end of the conversation Audrey realised she'd never shared so much of her past at once. Not with friends, and certainly not with a stranger. Perhaps it was the sense that she was trapped in the pub, that she couldn't leave till the police came to question her again; the only action she could take was some kind of confession. And also Noah had stung her by pointing out that he wasn't the only one keeping things back. She'd wanted to prove him wrong with her openness. The words had been waiting. It was just the listener who had changed.

And perhaps for the better. The woman had easy eyes and a calm face. She carried on the business of the pub, slicing lemons and filling the fridge, occasionally pausing their conversation to get someone a drink. Villagers came in, obviously wanting a chat with the landlady about last night's scandal. Somehow she always managed to divert them, and they ended up standing with their pints, talking to each other, occasionally flicking their eyes to the stranger at the end of the bar. Then she would come back to Audrey, nodding and asking small questions to get her story started again when it came to a halt.

But the end of the conversation came abruptly, in violent contrast to the slow unfolding Audrey had been making of herself. Griffin rushed in, the dog next to him barking in excitement. 'You'd better come quickly. Your fella's going to kill someone.'

CHAPTER 11

Preparations for the festival had clearly progressed. A pyre had been raised in the middle of the green, and surrounding it, like the standing stones in a prehistoric circle, were dozens of animals woven from branches and twigs: horses, rams, birds – or at least some of the parts of those creatures. And snakes. Among the other forms, sometimes with wings or horns, or jutting tongues, were the twining curves of many snakes.

Around the edges of the green, villagers were chatting or adjusting the positions of the obby osses. Or they would have been, had they not been distracted by the two men rolling on the ground fighting, tangled in each other and in the sculpture of a bird-beast they had knocked over.

The men were Cameron and Noah.

Audrey and Griffin had arrived running, but it was Reverend Pascoe who reached the fight first. She wasn't quick enough to separate them before Noah landed a hard punch. When Audrey pounded up, the vicar was pulling Noah off a stilled Cameron; blood leaked brightly from his mouth onto the grass. Lamorna was crying out, 'Trevor, no! You mustn't – oh.'

Noah turned, chest heaving, and looked at the vicar, whose usual flustered blush was now spreading over her cheeks. 'I mistook you for—'

'For Trevor?' said Griffin.

'It's just, from the back, I thought…'

Audrey tipped her head on one side and looked at Noah, squinting with her artist's eye to see the shape, not the man. It was true they had the same build, and Trevor, unlike Griffin, kept his hair cut short. If you ignored the clothes and saw them from behind, where the difference in skin colour wasn't evident, it would be possible to mistake one for the other. They even had a similar way of carrying themselves. But why would the Reverend Pascoe, who evidently knew Trevor well, make such a mistake?

The man on the ground spluttered a little and turned on his side. DI Morgan came lurching across the green, his usually genial face wearing a furious expression. 'You're coming with me,' he said, grabbing Noah by the collar. Noah's chest was heaving, and his hair was full of grass. His normally impeccable clothes were rumpled and disordered; he looked more like a local than she'd have thought possible. Audrey stared at him, perplexed. She wouldn't have thought he'd have a fight in him, let alone a knock-out punch.

'He accused me—'

'I don't care whether he said the moon was made from green cheese. I saw you hit him first, and look at the state of him!' DI Morgan was dragging Noah away, towards his car parked by the green. 'It's a night in the cells for you, Mr Dyer. And you'll be lucky if you don't do time for GBH.'

'Audrey!' Noah called to her. She wasn't sure what she could do, but she followed them, leaving Griffin bent over Cameron on the grass. Sergeant Varley was kneeling next to him, patting his back gently as he came round.

'What happened?' she asked breathlessly, trotting alongside Morgan and Noah. Yesterday's bonhomie was gone, and DI Morgan wrenched Noah along by the collar with no concern for his comfort. 'Please, DI Morgan. When they left the pub to talk, none of this was in the air.'

'He accused me of killing her!' said Noah, with the petulant outrage of a child finding something unfair.

'And you make it less believable by reacting like that?' replied Morgan. 'Last night was a closed book as far as I was concerned. Not any more.'

They were at the car now, and the policeman shoved Noah roughly into the back. Now who knows when we're going to get a chance to clarify where we stand, Audrey thought. Then she reprimanded herself for being focused on something as petty as relationship status. Noah had larger concerns.

'I didn't do it, Audrey,' he said through the open window. 'Nobody did. She killed herself.'

'I couldn't have done it. None of you understand.' He sank back into the seat and closed his eyes.

The car pulled away, and Audrey watched it go, wondering what to believe.

*

Around the green, people were knotted together, righting toppled statues and discussing the fight. Audrey saw them throw her dark looks. She knew what they were thinking: outsider. In the pub their looks had been merely curious, but now they were beginning to tip over into hostility. She felt hot and ashamed. None of this was her fault, and yet in the eyes of the village it was enough to be involved, enough to be implicated. Part of her wanted to face it out, to stalk off unconcerned and reappear at the evening's ceremony with her nose in the air, ostentatiously nonchalant. Then the old refrain of village life ran across her mind, faded but still buzzing faintly with its former power: *But what will people think?* She walked over to the knot that had formed around Cameron; although she wasn't that concerned for him, it would look right to pretend.

The cluster around him was less sympathetic than she'd expected. Lamorna Pascoe was knelt beside him, fussing without being useful. She kept saying 'Oh dear' and yanking at the grass like a child. Her black trousers were covered in torn green handfuls. Griffin was sitting back on his heels, watching. He gave Audrey a small nod. Varley was kneeling behind Cameron, hoisting him into a seated position. Other villagers were clustered around them, watching as Cameron moaned and held his head, making no move to help him. The dog nosed at him and he pushed it roughly away.

'They that wive between sickle and scythe...' said one man, dressed all in white with an embroidered blue belt tied round his waist. His clothes had a ceremonial look, and the words too made him seem like someone stepping out of the past. Those standing next to him tutted and nodded, and continued in rhyming unison: '…shall never thrive.'

'Less of that. Give him some room,' said the policeman, waving off the villagers with his hand.

Audrey moved closer as the others moved away. 'Are you all right?' she asked Cameron. He looked up at her, his eyes struggling to focus, blood smeared from nose to chin.

'Stay away from me. You and him. You ruined everything.' He lurched to his feet, arms windmilling towards her, and Audrey stepped back, alarmed – but he was only trying to make way. He burst through the ring of onlookers and staggered off, Varley following.

The Reverend Pascoe seemed shaken out of her stupor. She rose and brushed some of the grass from her trousers. 'I should make sure he isn't concussed,' she said, and followed the other two away from the green.

Griffin stood and took Audrey by the elbow. 'Come with me, Aud.'

'I told you not to call me that,' she said, pulling away.

He turned and started walking, as though there was no doubt she would follow. And Audrey did keep stumbling along behind him, too bewildered by the past twenty-four hours, not to mention the past twenty-four minutes, to do anything but follow someone who seemed to know what to do. Her sketchbook, jammed into the bottom of her bag, thwacked against her side with each hurried step. Now and then the dog looked back, as though checking she was still there.

They crossed the bridge and started up the river path, which was shaded by trees. Here Griffin's steps slowed and Audrey was able to pull even with him. He looked at her and smiled, rueful now he realised he'd been keeping up an antisocial speed. 'Sorry. I thought it was best to get out of there. I hate when there's drama in the village. Everyone gets together, starts gossiping. You can't get away from it.'

'I can't imagine what it was like growing up here.' She could, of course; her own village had been much the same.

'It's a good place, but it does feel small sometimes.'

'Have you never thought of leaving?'

'I did leave. I only came back a couple of years ago.'

This gave Audrey pause. She'd never thought about going back. But then Griffin's family wasn't hers. She thought of Morwenna, calmly curious, peacefully understanding. She was a person you'd be glad to see every day. 'Where did you go?'

'Where does anyone go when they're twenty-two and after an adventure? London.'

'Really?'

He smiled sidelong. 'So hard to believe?'

'Well, you seem to fit here.' Audrey's own relocation to London had involved deliberately changing as many aspects of her personality as she could: new clothes, new mannerisms, new start.

'I do and I don't. I told you already that there aren't that many people who look like me down here. There was a time when I thought it might be nice to blend in.'

'Or to get away?' Audrey asked, though she was thinking more of her own motives than his.

'Sure. But turns out that wanting to get away from something usually means you're going to bring whatever it is with you.'

This was painfully apt. Audrey's portfolio of dark drawings sprang to her mind.

'What did you do there? You seem to turn your hand to just about everything in the village. Cafe, taxi, pub dogsbody.'

'Most people down here pick up any bits of work going. But no, I had what you'd call a career in London. I worked in theatre.'

'What?' This time she stopped on the path, staring at him. There he stood, in his slouchy old clothes, his scruffy dog leaning against his leg, framed by the throbbing green of the freshly washed summer woods. When she thought how hard she worked to play the part of glamorous urban creative, and here was someone who'd done it and didn't need everyone to know. Comfortable in his own skin.

He was grinning at her, as usual, greatly amused by her surprise. 'You aren't the most tactful person, are you?'

'Sorry.' She started walking again. 'Were you an actor?'

He barked laughter. 'Not on your life. I did sets. Building, painting. You're not the only one who can draw, you know.'

'How do you know I draw?'

'Looked you up after I dropped you off yesterday.'

It could have been creepy, someone googling her like that. But it was so openly avowed, she found she didn't object. Was flattered, even. 'Wait, though – how? I don't have any reception down here. I figured everyone used a landline.'

He laughed. 'You really think we're in the back of beyond, don't you? Mobile reception can be spotty, I'll give you that, especially in a storm. But we do have this thing called the internet, I'm sure you city folk have heard of it. You can use the pub Wi-Fi when we get back.'

'Back from where?'

'From here.' He stepped to one side so she could see where he'd been leading her.

A while ago the path had bent away from the river. She'd thought they'd been heading deeper into the woods – strange that she hadn't hesitated to follow him, given how she generally felt about woods. But now she realised they'd been following a tributary, one of the many brooks and creeks that fed the river as it gathered pace flowing towards the sea. Griffin had guided her towards the head of this small thread of water. Now she stepped out from between the trees into a hollow made of leaves and branches, tumble-sided hills and mossy logs, and which held sunlight and singing water. No threatening shadows, just many-coloured light.

'You'll want to take off your shoes.'

Audrey pulled her gaze away from the green-gold sight and looked askance at Griffin; but he was pulling off his own trainers and she realised he was only inviting her in for a paddle. She hesitated, but the water, flowing clear out of the hillside and pooling around moss-velveted boulders before it continued towards the river, was irresistible. All that ominous talk in the village, about the river's tithe, had seemed silly. Yet it did seem to have a will of its own. And at this spot, it wanted to play.

She peeled off her socks and rolled up her jeans, embarrassed at the pallor of her naked feet, and then gasped when she stepped into the cold water. She and Griffin stood still, ankles submerged, toes wiggling, the dog, more animated, bouncing through the water around them. The spray caught her, and she laughed a little. A bird, disturbed by their presence, took off invisibly but audibly, calling a high repeated shriek, at once indignant and beautiful.

'That's—'

'A curlew,' she finished before Griffin could. He looked at her, one eyebrow cocked. 'Girl Guides,' she said, raising three fingers in salute.

He didn't comment, just smiled. A smile, not a grin. She smiled back. And felt, for the first time since she wasn't sure when, completely unworried about what anyone thought.

CHAPTER 12

They returned to the village. Audrey thought she had better get back to the pub in case DI Morgan turned up to question her. She felt shy again as they retraced their steps in silence, but deliciously so – not self-conscious, but self-aware.

As they approached the pub, Audrey noticed its wooden sign for the first time. Above the elegant serif capitals of the Saracen's Head was a head, painted onto a pale round that might have been an ornate silver dish or an Elizabethan ruff – the head of a black woman with open eyes, looking calmly at the viewer. A striped snake arched over her across a twilit sky.

'It's your mum!' said Audrey in sudden surprise.

'Good, isn't it?' said Griffin with relish. 'Though I say so myself. When we were at school, we tried to persuade her to change the name to something less offensive, but she always said she took it as a sign the place was waiting for her. So I painted that to replace the old one.'

Inside, Audrey tapped the Wi-Fi password into her phone, feeling a bit silly that she hadn't previously noticed it written

prominently in chalk behind the bar. A dozen notifications popped up, texts and emails, almost all from Jemima:
Just wondering about the images...
Can you meet the next deadline?
Don't they have reception in France?!
She groaned.
'Everything okay?'
'Yes and no. Nobody's died. Except my career.'

DI Morgan found Audrey in the pub, sketching. In her panic about work, she'd forgotten all about speaking to him. She was furious with herself for the way her mind kept drifting away from hedgerow charm and on to the horrors and oddities she'd seen in the past few days. For every bright-eyed bunny she managed to get down on the page, another image escaped from somewhere deeper and darker: Cameron's stupefied and bloody face, a desiccated sculpture of a snake.

'We need to talk.'

Audrey was annoyed to be interrupted, having conceived a mad hope that she could pacify Jemima with some photos of these drafts. Still, she'd known he'd have questions for her, after everything that had happened. She tucked her pencil into her sketchbook and folded it away, trying not to let her reluctance show. 'Should I come with you to the station or something?'

'This is an informal conversation. And I could use this,' he said, raising the glass he'd brought over with him.

'Should you be drinking on duty?' Audrey asked, then regretted it immediately. But he didn't take offence.

'Regulations state that a half of best bitter is permitted to officers over fifty. All part of the retention drive. Be a riot otherwise.' He took a placid sip.

There was a wink in all this. And she was pretty sure he shouldn't be questioning her in a pub. But then she thought of his firm grip on Noah, dragging him away from the fight, and the time he'd taken looking at the details of the scene where they'd found Stella. Perhaps the rumpled, avuncular informality was a way of disarming people. DI Morgan could be very much the policeman when he chose.

'How did you leave Noah?' she asked.

He settled in the chair across from her. 'He's cooling off in town. We're holding him for now, but it depends what Cameron Grant says about the fight. And what you say.'

'What *I* say? I didn't see it. I was in here. I mean, I can tell you Noah's never done anything like that, that I know of. Skinny boys who work in galleries aren't known for starting fist fights.' But even as she came to his defence, she realised her loyalty was instinctual – did she really know him?

'It's not the fight I was wanting to ask you about. I'm sure an observant girl like you would give a good account if you could, but we've got plenty of witnesses from the green, people who were there before it started. Don't worry about that.'

Morgan came to a stop and seemed unsure how to proceed. He leaned forward and tapped his hands on his knees, opening his mouth a couple of times without speaking. Then he looked around and his gaze settled on the picture above the fireplace.

'A drink with Cousin Jack,' he said softly, reading the caption.

Audrey recognised her own stalling tactic from her earlier conversation with Noah. 'What did you want to ask about then?' she prodded.

He pulled his attention away from the picture. 'It goes further back a bit. I hate to make you relive a terrible night, but…' He looked round, as though nervous of being overheard. A few tables were surrounded by villagers, discussing recent events with too much excitement to listen to anyone else's conversation, though now and again they looked over at Audrey and the detective. The three Kingcups were together behind the bar, doing brisk business.

'You want to ask about what happened last night.'

'It might be helpful to go over that again, yes. And further back. I wanted to enquire about your reasons for coming here. About what was at the bottom of the trip, you might say.'

Audrey didn't mention how many times in the past two days she'd wondered the same thing. She merely said that Noah had planned it, a romantic weekend, and she thought he'd chosen Cornwall because of a childhood holiday. 'I'd have preferred Paris,' she couldn't help adding.

'See, here is where the questions arise,' said Morgan, 'because your man says he was the one who wanted to go to Paris, and you insisted on the West Country.'

'What?'

'This trip was your idea.'

'But it wasn't.'

Audrey was aware that her flat denial sounded just that – flat. She was so taken aback by Noah's lie that she didn't know how else to respond. What could have possessed him? What did the lie serve? Whatever other questions it cast up, one thing was clear: after this, it was over. How could he lie about this and bring her into it?

'Are you sure? Making plans, buying tickets – sometimes we forget where it started.'

'Look at his emails. I haven't booked a thing, it was Noah who arranged the tickets, who rented the house. Or the room, anyway. He rented it from Cameron, so they should both have emails to prove it. I have nothing, I wasn't involved.'

'Ah well, that's good then. I like a paper trail.' He resumed kneading his splayed thighs, but with a relieved air.

'Why does it matter anyway? I mean, we just happened to be visiting at an unfortunate time, we weren't involved in what happened. It was a suicide.'

'So it was. And there's many in the village would be satisfied with that explanation. Call it a superstition, if you like, but there's folks here think you shouldn't put your own celebrations above the festival. The river, the land – they make their own demands. The two at the big house were meant to marry in a month's time. There was a big celebration planned, and some might say she was being put in her place by the river.'

So that was what the villager had meant by 'They that wive'. 'Is that what you think?'

'I'm a local lad, it can't be denied.' He ran a finger round his collar. 'At the same time, I'm a policeman. Don't see a lot of river gods had up in the dock.'

'And, as a policeman, are you satisfied it was a suicide?'

'I am and I'm not. On the one hand, a woman is found with a knife in her neck, her own hand round it, in a locked room whose window gives onto a cliff face. That locked room is itself in a house with transparent walls, where anyone coming or going would have been seen. Some round here might mutter that the river put it in her head. More likely is something private that we don't know of. Suicide seems the clear explanation.'

'I don't have your expertise,' said Audrey, 'but I would have thought so too.'

Morgan nodded, staring at the floor and musing, absently chewing his lips. Then he looked up and met her gaze. 'And yet. Stella Penrose wasn't a woman you'd have thought would take her own life. I can't say as I was her friend, and there's always more to people's lives than you see on the surface. But this is a small place, full of people who knew her as a girl. Her character wasn't in doubt – she was a proud woman, she thought well of herself, and it isn't usually such people who meet such ends. And her circumstances are well known. She was wealthy, she had a fine career that brought her praise and excitement. She was marrying soon, a strapping young man. She had projects. Reckon in her position you'd want to stab yourself?'

'But isn't a suicide always shocking? Even when a much more desperate person than Stella takes their life, we say they had so much to live for.' Audrey was thinking of her own life, which showed that all kinds of things could remain hidden, however small the place – though did people really not know what went on, or did they choose to ignore it?

'People say that. But it isn't always true. Underneath the shock, people aren't usually that surprised.'

'It doesn't change the fact that she was in a locked room, glass doors, all the rest of it.'

'You make a good point. But still, something doesn't smell right.' Morgan took a considering sip. 'I'd feel easier if I could find a motive. A suicide needs a motive, like any other murder.'

'Perhaps you'll uncover something. Debts, maybe? Her show being cancelled? Something that came as a blow. Perhaps her life wasn't as fabulous as it seemed.'

'It's possible. But we might also uncover something that helps us see clearer the other way.'

Something about the way he said this made Audrey ask, 'Have you?'

Morgan looked round at the Kingcups, still clustered by the bar, at rest now the post-fight rush had passed. Griffin and Morwenna were speaking, their tone low enough that Audrey couldn't make out their words. Trevor was quiet, staring moodily down at his hands, splayed on the dark wood, but he seemed to be listening to his family, not to them. When DI Morgan spoke, he didn't answer Audrey's question directly.

'If you take all those reasons to live, and you combine them with a couple of other factors, a certain, well, uncertainty begins to enter the case. For one thing, there's the angle of the blade.' He demonstrated with his own hand, raising it to neck height and shaping it in a grip round an imaginary knife. 'If you or I, God forbid, were to go about such a grim task, we'd probably hold it like this, stabbing ourselves on the opposite side to the hand holding the knife, with the wrapped fingers facing downwards. Or perhaps like this, on the same side, but with the wrapped fingers facing back behind us. What we wouldn't do,' he continued, shifting the position of his hand each time to make it clear, 'is stab ourselves on the opposite side but with the fingers facing in towards the neck. Try it, you'll see what I mean.'

Audrey twisted her own hand into the same position, brought it across her body and in towards her neck, finishing with the side of her hand resting on her collarbone and the thumb angled out and away, as she had seen Stella's when they found her body. Then she moved her hand into the other positions, as Morgan had demonstrated. 'Your wrist's weaker. You don't have the same leverage,' she said.

'Exactly. Now, I don't say it's not possible to force the knife in that way. It is. But it's damned awkward, and I don't see why you would, if you were already determined to bring yourself to that sort of end.'

'I agree it's awkward, but is it enough to create uncertainty?'

'Another factor, and I hope you won't take it badly my saying so, is yourself.'

'Me?' Her tone rose sharply, and Trevor looked over at them.

'You and your man, taken together. Now, you've pointed me towards the evidence that this trip wasn't your idea,'

Morgan said, holding up a hand to prevent any further protest, 'and I'm satisfied that if we look into it we'll find what you said we'd find. But you can't deny that it muddles things, two strangers turning up right around the time the tragedy happens. Especially when they have different stories regarding why they're there. And even more especially when one of them ends up in a fight with the deceased woman's fiancé, after certain accusations are made.'

Audrey had sunk further into her chair as he said this, an anxious flush creeping over her body. She knew she'd done nothing wrong, but she also knew how it sounded. And she was sure Trevor was listening now. His glare at the counter had deepened.

'If I'm so suspicious, why are you telling me all this?'

'First of all, because you don't do police work as long as I have without getting an instinct for people, and I have a good feeling about you.'

The detective smiled gently at her, and in spite of everything Audrey found herself smiling back. She thought of Morwenna earlier, making a similar claim about the knowledge of human nature you developed working in a pub. She, too, seemed to have a good feeling about Audrey. It was strange; all she'd done since she'd arrived in this place was get caught up in scandals and loudly announce her wish to leave. And yet DI Morgan, Morwenna, even Griffin in his irritating way, seemed to like having her around.

'And second of all?'

The detective sighed. 'Second of all is something I shouldn't tell you, and don't want to tell you. But you might be one of the only people who can shed any light on the matter.' He ground to a halt, looking down at his hands, making a basket of his fingers as though to put off what he had to say. Audrey felt a bit sick. She wished he wouldn't draw it out.

'If you're going to tell me, tell me.'

'We found something in the bin in Stella Penrose's bedroom. Another factor for uncertainty, you could say.'

'Yes? What?'

'We found a condom.' He looked pained as he said it, but he carried on delivering further blows. 'Used. Evidently quite recently. Earlier on the same day she died, in fact. And her fiancé had left the day before.'

CHAPTER 13

Audrey reached for her glass, then realised it was empty. She slowly replaced it on the low table in front of her, making sure the base of the glass lined up perfectly with the moisture ring which marked where it had stood before. She knew there were implications waiting somewhere to be understood. But she couldn't see them yet. She sat in her forgiving armchair, sinking into its worn leather recesses, looking at DI Morgan. There was a watchful glitter in his eye as he looked back at her.

Then, a word: Noah.

Ah, yes. That was it. The thing waiting on the edge of vision, the edge of consciousness. The realisation that exactly what she'd suspected, the thing he'd so vehemently denied, was true. Because who else could have slept with Stella in the time between the departure of her fiancé and the moment she died?

It must have been Noah. Noah, who'd assured her that she'd got it all wrong. In fact, it had been much worse than she'd feared. Not just a flirtation, insensitively carried out in front of her, but an actual betrayal. He'd gone into the woman's room while she was sleeping across the hall – behind nothing but glass and a filmy curtain, practically in plain view – and cheated on Audrey.

To sleep with someone else in the room next to hers, while she slept off the wine she'd drunk too much of precisely because he was ignoring her, was horrific. To tell her she was imagining things when he came back from doing it was possibly even worse. And then to cap it all off, he had cast blame on her in the eyes of the police. If he could betray her like that, what else was he capable of?

DI Morgan shifted in his own chair opposite, evidently waiting for a response. She looked over at the bar. Morwenna was serving a couple of villagers, both wearing white with blue sashes round their waists. Griffin and his brother had melted away.

'Do you think this means…' She cleared her throat and had another run at it. 'Do you think this means Noah and Stella…' She still couldn't finish, but it didn't matter; Morgan could follow her train of thought.

'Is that what you thought it meant?'

'Thought? But you've only just told me about it.'

'Of course, of course.' He cleared his throat, but didn't move on quickly enough to cover the implication. He'd just tried to catch Audrey out, on the off-chance that she'd killed Stella, motivated by a jealous rage.

'You don't seriously think I had anything to do with it?' she asked, almost too shocked to be angry.

'You have to admit all possibilities in my line of work,' he said, 'whatever you hope is true.' The watchful glitter had become a twinkle again. He was slyer than he looked, Morgan. The rumpled, friendly air, the sharing of confidential information – and then it turned out he'd been laying a trap all along. 'You can't confirm, then...'

'I can't.'

He nodded and put his hands up to indicate he wouldn't push. 'It's possible the... item was there before you two arrived, of course. Unfortunately it was mishandled when they were bagging up the scene, and we can't count on a DNA reading. So we're trying to piece together a timeline. But we don't know of any visitors to her house after Cameron Grant's departure the day before, and he said he knew she didn't have anything in the diary.'

'Of course, she wouldn't tell him about it if she were going to see someone behind his back.' Audrey seized on this hope; it didn't entirely assuage the quicksand feeling inside her, but it was something to cling to.

'The possibility certainly remains open. But given that we know of one male visitor to the house during the window we're looking at, it's, ah, difficult not to concentrate on him, and on what he might have been doing.'

'Yes, I'm finding it hard not to think about that too,' Audrey replied with a rather bitter smile.

'And yet,' he said, leaning forward and speaking in a confidential tone, 'if I'm really honest with you, here's what I think—'

He sat up quickly. Lamorna was coming over. She was looking hotter and more bothered than ever, imprisoned in her unsummery black. 'Paul, I need to speak to you,' she said. 'We've found something.' They both looked at Audrey – Morgan apologetically, the vicar expectantly – until she took the hint and moved away.

Morwenna had come out from behind the bar and was leaning against the open door of the pub, looking out, her face shaded by the vines that twined over the entrance. The sun was strong, a few degrees down from its apex, and the air outside was thick and steamy, last night's storm still evaporating off the grass here and there.

Audrey joined her, thinking that now she was out from behind the bar, she wasn't as expected. From Griffin's comments about Morwenna's sixth sense, and the unexpected urge to confide she had caused, not to mention the fact that this was Cornwall, Audrey would have guessed she'd be sporting a peasant skirt or something home-made: the garb of an earth mother. But Morwenna was wearing trainers, jeans and a Breton top, like any woman you might see by the coast in summer.

'Just a few more hours. It'll start as soon as the sun sets.' She didn't look over as she said it, and Audrey felt caught out – she'd been observed observing.

'What will?'

'The ritual.'

'Ritual? Not festival?'

'To you it's a festival, maybe. To those of us who live here, it's more of a rite.'

'What's the difference?'

'How much you care.'

'And you care a lot?'

Now the older woman turned to look at her, nodding slowly, wearing a faint smile. 'Life's wheels have to be made to run smoothly on their tracks. If you don't grease them…'

'What happens?'

Audrey thought of the villagers shaking their heads over Cameron. *They that wive between sickle and scythe shall never thrive.* She felt sorry for him, betrayed by a woman who was dead, tutted at by the community. And what did Morwenna mean by 'greasing the wheels'? Her face was kind and calm; Audrey instinctively trusted her. But was that just the calm of the true believer? Was the placidity actually coldness? Audrey had been making jokes about Wicker Man-style sacrifices since she came down here, but the way people talked about the river's due, it almost seemed like they believed in that kind of bloodthirsty cosmic balance.

'Better not to find out, isn't it?'

'There must have been a year where nobody bothered.'

Morwenna shook her head. 'Other places down here stopped a long time ago – all those bonfires seemed dangerous, I suppose. Modern life entertains in other ways. Some of them have started up again. You can go there if you want to see a "festival". But here we never stopped, and who knows if it's the reason, but the place never died either.'

'What do you mean, the place never died?'

'You know a dead place when you see one. Young people all gone, shops shuttered. There are a lot of them down here, zombie places, only kept alive by visitors. Whereas our place… Come here.' Morwenna waved her over, and Audrey took a step closer, sharing the view of the sloping village green, the narrow stone bridge, the villagers gathering in their white clothes, all under strong afternoon light. Morwenna raised a pointing hand. 'See the trees lining the river? No ash dieback. See the people on the green? All ages. In the old days my family were smugglers – publicans often were, keeping barrels of cognac in the tunnels, winking about "Cousin Jack". But we never got caught. My son's mussel farm on the estuary gives good, sweet, clean mussels every year. We're not the only pretty village in the county, but you go and see how many of them are thriving. We always give the river her due, and she gives us back, see.'

'But I thought your sons couldn't find anywhere to rent? They had to move back in with you?'

'Exactly.' Morwenna nodded in satisfaction, her point proved. 'Where else would always have a home for them?'

Audrey smiled, not wholly convinced by this circular argument. The phrase *true believer* drifted across her mind again. 'So what does it entail, this ritual that's kept Trevennick safe for so many centuries?'

'This is the first night. Tonight we appease the river. Tomorrow we defy it.'

'Defy it? Surely that's the opposite of what you want to do?'

'Everything in this world is a balance. We live on the river, depend on it. It's the most important thing in our world. So, on the first night we give it gifts, we show it that we're grateful. And on the second night we remind it that it also needs us. We make our stand. Respect goes two ways.'

'How exactly do you tell it all these things?'

'Simple ways – fire and water, statues and masks, dancing, singing. Taking the time to reaffirm our bond.'

They both looked out on the view in silence for a while. The green was crowded with obby osses now. Men and women, girls and boys, all wearing white clothes and blue embroidered sashes, walked among the sculptures, carefully repositioning the serpents and rams according to an inscrutable design. It was a charming sight, or at least it should have been. There was just something about those animals that she didn't like. Audrey couldn't tell if she found it chilling because she sensed some dark undercurrent to the proceedings, or if it was only her old hostility to rural life, its sun-drenched boredom, its collusions and silences. She shivered and asked, 'Why are the creatures all wrong, though? It's all horsefish and birdsnakes.'

'What's a birdsnake but a dragon?' replied Morwenna, which Audrey found neither illuminating nor reassuring. She tried to assert the rational modern view.

'Couldn't it just be that having a tradition everyone participates in keeps the village community strong? And so people stay, and it thrives, but not because some river god has been appeased?'

Morwenna shrugged. 'You can give a sociological explanation, sure. And Tom Cartwright over there' – she pointed to one of the men on the green, the one who'd muttered 'They that wive' – 'would insist it's all about the songs, and give you a lecture about folk music traditions in the West Country. Whichever way you cut it, though, it comes back to the ritual being a good thing. The truth wears all kinds of clothes.'

A thirsty villager, tired of heaving obby osses about in the sun, approached the door, and Morwenna smiled at Audrey and moved off to serve him. As they went inside, she heard him saying, 'This death up at the big house, now...'

Audrey was tempted to move closer, to listen to how the villagers discussed things between themselves, but then Trevor approached her. He stood in the doorway where his mother had been, looking out at the same view, but without the same peaceful expression. She wondered briefly if his brows ever unknit themselves.

'She been telling you how perfect everything is down here?'

'Something like that. You sound like you don't agree.'

He shrugged. 'My mother's a very perceptive woman. But also a selective one. She sees what she wants to see sometimes.'

'Griffin said you didn't have such an easy time of it, growing up here.'

'School's school.' He waved the past away. 'The problem now is the way the place is changing. My mother thinks doing things as we've always done them will keep us safe. But no ritual is going to stop run-off from a new development poisoning my mussels. Or make the rents affordable for locals, instead of developers selling off the houses to Londoners who want a place by the seaside.'

'Careful, I'll think you resent people like me coming down here.' But it had been wrong to try levity with him; he only looked at her, there was no smile, nor any contradiction. Perhaps resented was exactly what he wanted her to feel.

'Nobody knows better than me the beauty of this place. Nobody loves it like me.' He spoke with ferocity, his hands shoved deep in his pockets, a heel tapping rapidly against the floor. 'And I won't let it be ruined. Not by anyone.'

'I'm sure you won't.'

Audrey didn't have any intention of ruining it. She just wanted to get away. But the way he spoke, the idea that she was in his cross hairs somehow, that frightened her.

DI Morgan came up behind them and Trevor moved off with another dark look at her. The policeman put a hand on Audrey's shoulder. 'I have to go talk to that foolish boy Noah Dyer again. But don't you worry, I think I know how to get him out of this. He's done himself no favours. But I can see what's happened here.'

Then he was off, leaving Audrey unsure what he had meant. Was Noah a foolish boy for sleeping with Stella? Or for something else? And shouldn't she be more relieved at the thought that he might be innocent after all?

CHAPTER 14

She wanted to ask Lamorna what she'd found, what she'd told the detective to send him off in such a hurry. But the other woman had followed him quickly out of the pub, and Audrey was left staring after them, uncertain. A wave of desolation swept over her – she didn't want to be here, caught in this miserable situation.

But then what was waiting for her at home? A messy flat, and a tidy studio. Undone work and unanswered emails. She probably didn't even have a boyfriend any more. She'd thought, when she and Noah started dating and then she had her first real success, that things were finally working out for her. Now, a few months later, the opposite seemed true. She was alone, letting her career fall apart, and embroiled in the investigation of a suspicious death. She had a house to go back to, but nothing that made it home. Just her eighteen-year-old self's idea of what she'd make her life into, gradually wearing away like a chalk picture drawn on the pavement.

'You look as sad as I've ever seen you.' Griffin had come up next to her while she was lost in thought. She tried to muster up a smile.

'You haven't seen me very much.'

'True.' He nodded and picked a leaf off the vine next to his face, holding it up and twirling it against the light. 'But you've been pretty unhappy that whole time.'

She was taken aback. It was one thing to know he'd been watching her, another thing to feel he'd been seeing. 'It's definitely not what anyone would plan for their holiday.'

'Of course not. But that's not really the problem, is it?'

It was true that she'd been thinking along the same lines moments ago, but what gave him the right? She straightened up, brushed past him, then turned, unable to resist the temptation to give him a piece of her mind. 'I don't know you. Whatever's right or wrong in my life has nothing to do with you. You can keep your thoughts about my problems to yourself.'

'So you don't want me to tell you what Lamorna Pascoe and DI Morgan were talking about?' he replied, wearing that infuriating grin.

Audrey cursed herself, but couldn't help taking the bait. 'Did you overhear?'

'Not really – but wait.' She was turning to go, making a disgusted face at his ploy, but he caught her arm and held her back. 'I didn't need to. I'm almost certain I know what she told him.'

'Well? Spill. And if you don't have anything to say this time, I'm leaving.'

'It was about Noah.'

'Obviously.'

Griffin scrubbed his face with his hands. It was the first time Audrey had seen him frustrated. 'This isn't the easiest thing to say…' he began.

Audrey waited for him to continue. But they were still standing in the doorway, and some sort of exodus from the village green began, with villager after villager pushing past them to get into the pub. Most of them inspected Audrey closely as they passed. If she went back inside, she knew a silence would fall, as everyone left off talking about the Londoners there at the big house when Stella Penrose died. Thinking about it made her neck prickle.

'We can't talk here. Follow me.' Griffin took her hand again and led her around the side of the building. There, a staircase rose through the overhanging grapevines and wisteria, leading to a door above. Griffin's hand was warm and dry, and he didn't let go even though she was following behind. The dog trotted next to them.

Inside, she realised where they were – the flat the Kingcups lived in. The hallway was a tumble of wellies, shoes, dog toys and bags, the kind of mess that had always suggested a happy family to Audrey, in contrast to her own claustrophobically tidy childhood home.

Griffin's room was neater than the hall, but still cluttered. Rolled-up canvases and bits of painted scenery were stacked against the walls, presumably leftovers from his time in London. A fleecy dog bed sat on the floor at the foot of his own bed, which was pushed against the wall, and the animal settled into it with a sigh. Out of the window you could see the decorated green, the river and the woods beyond.

'Sit, please.' He waved at the bed and she sat gingerly down on the blue cotton sheets. A faint boyish smell wafted up – human, not unpleasant.

Griffin thrust his hands in his pockets and took a breath, struggling to begin. He looked more like his brother in this darker mood. Audrey could trace their common gestures, as well as the resemblance of feature. She resisted getting out her sketchbook and waited for him to speak.

'I think Noah and I are brothers.'

Of all the things he could have said, she would never have predicted this. She was too shocked to respond at first, and even the dog seemed startled, raising and cocking his head. Eventually words began to emerge, a babble of incomplete questions.

'How… and why do you… but you don't look—'

'Anything like each other?' He smiled, lighter-hearted again now he'd launched himself into what he had to say. 'But we do. I mean, there's an obvious difference. Most people wouldn't look beyond that.' Audrey looked down, shamed by the thought that no, she hadn't even considered that they looked like each other. 'But our dad was white. And we've all got certain traits, Noah and Trevor and me – height, build, some of our facial features. We all look like our dad.'

Audrey remembered Lamorna's mistake on the green, and squinting and seeing the same outline on the two men. 'Okay, I can see that. But lots of people look like each other. Do you go around assuming every man your size and height is related to you?'

'Of course not. But I always thought someone like him might be out there.'

'Why?'

'Our dad left when I was a baby. Trevor was older, he saw what was going on and explained it to me when I grew up a little. He didn't go because he and my mum couldn't get along. He had an affair.'

'An affair that led to…'

'Maybe. It's not something Mum's ever given us a straight answer about.'

Audrey nodded, considering. 'Okay. I can see why you might be on the lookout for your long-lost brother. And I can see that Noah's a possible fit, physically. But what makes it more than a possibility? You sounded pretty sure.'

'Because…' Griffin cleared his throat and turned to the window again. He reached a hand up to run through his hair. Audrey noticed a slice of flesh become visible at his waist as his T-shirt rose up with his hand, and then wondered why she'd noticed. 'Because the affair was with Stella Penrose.'

The pressure of the words turned a wheel in her mind; the teeth of various cogs connected, the machine was set spinning, and for the first time in two days Audrey felt something clicking into place. 'Stella Penrose had an affair with your dad?'

'Yes.'

'An affair which possibly led to a child.'

'We think maybe.'

'After which your dad disappeared.'

'Well, *disappeared* is a bit strong. He left. We didn't see him for a while. He came back a few times for short visits. He kicked about various places on the coast, then, when I was in my teens, he died. He'd slipped into bad habits, drinking. He was never a very together person.'

'I'm sorry.'

Griffin shrugged. 'It's a sad thing. Harder for Trevor. He remembered the days when Dad was around. But we had our mum, and she's definitely as good as two average parents.'

Audrey smiled at his loyalty. She, too, felt there was something very soothing about Morwenna Kingcup's presence. 'So what did Stella do? Did she stay?'

'She disappeared around the same time Dad left. No one in the village heard a peep from her until she suddenly popped up on our television screens.'

'That must have been a shock for your mother.'

He nodded. 'I was just a kid, and I didn't remember our dad ever being here. Then one night this lady came on telly to talk about Celtic animal cults, and Mum froze. She sort of disappeared inside herself for a few minutes. Trevor thought she'd had a stroke. Eventually she woke up, burst into tears and ran out of the room. Not like her at all. It was terrifying for us. If he hadn't been so scared I don't think Trevor would have told me what he knew.' He turned away, moving about the room in silence.

Audrey thought about Morwenna's calm grace. If her son had developed this theory, she must have guessed at the possibility, and yet she hadn't shown any resentment towards

Noah in the pub, nor any exultation over Stella's death. Even Lamorna Pascoe, with her vocational duty to forgive, had been unable to resist enumerating the dead woman's faults. And how compassionate had Audrey herself been towards Noah or Stella, how able to set aside her own petty concerns? She felt shamed by Morwenna's magnanimity.

Griffin started flipping through the leaning pile of stacked stage scenery: a flowering bush, a crescent moon, a red door. Audrey prodded him to continue his story.

'So Trevor explained.'

'As much as he understood. Which wasn't much. But he remembered Stella being around when he was little – they were friends, her and our parents, they all grew up together. And there was talk in the village. He overheard enough to build a working theory, anyway.'

'That explains the way he talked about her earlier. The anger.'

Griffin looked at her in silence, perhaps afraid of the conclusions she might leap to next. When he spoke, there was a carefulness to his tone she hadn't heard before.

'It was harder for him. He had to become the man of the house. He took the brunt of gossip, of all kinds of ridicule I never had to put up with. He remembered what we'd lost. And then, when she came back this last couple of years, bought the big house, started talking about what she'd do with the land, it didn't exactly sit lightly on the village.'

'So the woman who destroyed his family returned, and she was rich and successful and not afraid to throw her weight around.'

Griffin winced, recognising that he'd led her towards an even more damning picture of his brother's feelings. 'Yeah. But it doesn't mean he'd... he wouldn't. I know him. He might be a moody bugger, but he's not violent.'

'She killed herself. It's the only explanation.'

'I guess.'

They were quiet, pondering. Nobody seemed to believe she had died by her own hand. And yet Audrey felt sure nothing else could have happened; the room had been locked from the inside, the knife was in her hand. But Griffin probably knew his brother better than anyone. She didn't know Noah better than anyone, but she knew him better than the people here did, and she didn't think he was a killer. And yet here they all were, tangled up in something none of them could see clearly. When Griffin had started talking, she'd thought she understood now – Noah's caginess had found its explanation. But the muddle was bigger than that, and it had yet to be resolved.

'So what do you think?' asked Griffin, coming to sit by her on the bed.

'I don't know what to think. Everything seems like a dead end. Stella killed herself, only she wouldn't have. Your brother hated her, but he wouldn't kill. Noah—'

'That's what I mean. Do you think it's possible he's our brother?' In spite of the ugly mess, there was hope in his voice.

She looked at him, touched. Whatever other perturbing truths would emerge from the situation, he wanted to know if he'd found part of his family. 'Well, yes. Noah wouldn't tell me much about why we were here – he sort of brought me down on false pretences, and then wouldn't explain why he was acting so weird around Stella.'

'That's when it occurred to me! His reaction when she came out of the house was so strong, and then I saw our dad in him all of a sudden. I tried not to get carried away, but there was something there, right?'

Audrey nodded. 'It was plain to see she meant something to him, even if I came up with, ah, other reasons for it before you told me this.'

'What other reasons?'

'You know. She was very flirty with him, in front of me. And he sort of... took it.'

'You thought they were going to sleep together?' Griffin made a face of equal amusement and disgust. Audrey was a bit prickled by the implication that she'd been silly, and in her pique decided to make her own revelation.

'We had a fight after we went to bed. We kind of half broke up. That, combined with the way they'd been acting towards each other – it made sense. Especially when DI Morgan told me that Stella had slept with someone before she died. But after Cameron left town.'

'Oh.' She had the satisfaction of seeing shock on Griffin's face. 'But surely they wouldn't, if they were...'

'I hope not. Maybe they didn't know.' She shuddered a little at the sordidness of it all. 'But I can't see who else Stella would have slept with. Still, Noah wouldn't do that. He's a bit cagey and withholding, but he's not sick. And I know one thing about his childhood that goes a long way to proving your theory.'

'What's that?'

'Noah was adopted.'

He sighed, and she felt the tension leaving his body next to her. 'I thought I was going crazy,' he said. 'But I bet I'm right.'

'I guess only Noah could confirm it for us. Or Stella. But yeah, I think you might be.'

'Stella must have got pregnant, and then gone away to have the baby. And then she stayed away, went to university, made her new life.'

'And maybe Noah found out who his mother was, and came down here to meet her. I'm not sure why he brought me along, though.'

'Do you think she knew too?' Griffin asked.

'No. She obviously felt something – if you'd seen them at dinner together… But I think he was waiting to tell her. He must have wanted to test the waters before he revealed who he really was.'

'So she died not knowing. How sad.'

'Yes. Unless…' Now Audrey was the one hesitating, reluctant to lead him where her thoughts had already gone.

'Unless?'

'Unless he did reveal the truth, and learning it had something to do with her death.'

'Huh.' Griffin considered this possibility, nodding slowly as he saw its sense. 'I guess the shock of it, maybe guilt too, suddenly all these things from her past were right there, confronting her.'

'Maybe. But that doesn't seem like the kind of reaction I'd expect from her.'

Griffin gave a small, rueful laugh. 'No, she was the type to take what she wanted and damn the consequences.'

'It's not as if Noah has turned out terribly. She was quite taken by him. If anything, I'm sure she'd be proud of him. Though she might have been upset if she realised she was flirting with him.'

'Maybe. Maybe the suicide would make more sense if she had slept with him. But if it didn't go further than a bit of banter, who on earth was with Stella between Cameron's departure and your arrival?'

'I was hoping you could tell me.'

He shrugged, bewildered. 'I know I'm from the village and everything, but honestly, your guess is as good as mine.'

'What about DI Morgan?' said Audrey, entirely unseriously. 'Maybe he's been running interference!'

'Can you imagine?' Griffin's eyes were wide, and although there wasn't anything funny about the situation, Audrey found herself laughing at the exaggerated shock on his face. Soon he was flushed and shaking too. 'I feel like I'm trying to shave with one eye closed or something.'

'Using your reflection in a polluted lake.'

'During stormy weather.'

'With no razor.'

And then, in the midst of their laughter, they leaned in closer to each other and kissed.

They kept kissing. It felt – well, it felt wonderful, and completely natural, and Audrey realised a few moments in that they'd both been thinking about doing it since they met at the station. How else to explain the fact that they fit perfectly, as though they'd been practising for each other, every subtle shift of pressure and rhythm desired and in tune? She didn't want to stop, this was much the nicest thing that had happened to her in... maybe ever. But eventually the dog whined and they came up for air, giving each other and the animal sheepish looks.

'I've, uh, I've wanted to do that for a while,' said Griffin, putting an embarrassed hand to the back of his head.

'It felt like it,' Audrey replied. 'I did too, obviously. I just didn't realise, because you're so annoying.'

He laughed. 'Classic schoolboy flirtation technique.'

She leaned in again. Their mouths met, and it felt hungrier, like they might keep going, unbutton each other and... but the dog gave another whine, and Audrey pulled away. 'We've got an audience,' she said, smiling. Griffin smiled back. She leaned into him, nestling under his chin. His arms came up easily around her. 'This feels good. You knew straight away?'

'I knew I liked the look of you. But you don't know until you know, you know?' They giggled. 'Plus, you have a boyfriend. Maybe.'

'Noah.' She slumped back against the wall, deflated by the reminder. After he'd thrown her under the bus with Morgan, not to mention the way he'd handled everything that had happened down here, it seemed likely things were over between them. But neither of them had said the words. And the Audrey of two days ago had been more or less happily in love, or at least committed to convincing herself she was. How could she already be sure about somebody new? Especially when that somebody had their own reasons to be interested in her ex.

'Hmmm. Noah. Shit.' His face went ashen and Audrey's heartbeat quickened, less agreeably now.

'What?'

'I can't steal my brother's girlfriend, can I?'

She looked at him, trying to read whether this was sincere. He was half-smiling, but there was a worried quirk to his brows. She straightened up. 'Hang on, a second ago you're all over me, and now you think my involvement with Noah is a problem?' She'd been thinking it was a problem for her, but somehow it felt less justified the other way around.

'I don't know, it's not a great way to get off on the right foot with him, is it?'

'You're not stealing anybody. Not yet. And we're as good as broken up.'

'As good as? Or broken up?'

This was too uncomfortably close to her own train of thought. She cast about for something else. 'Also, he's been arrested in circumstances connected with the suspicious death of a woman who's possibly his mother.'

'But you said you didn't think he'd done anything.'

'I don't. But I don't really know, do I? Nor do you. I mean, maybe there's something to do with inheritance, maybe he did have a reason to hurt Stella. The point is, now's not a great time to be worrying about building a relationship with your long-lost brother, is it?'

'If something's important it doesn't become less so because it's not a good time.'

'Are you talking about what happened with us, or what might happen with Noah?'

'Jesus, Audrey. I don't know. We just met. I mean, what do you want me to say?'

'Something better than that.' She was being petulant, she knew it. But she couldn't stop herself. Some part of her wanted him to be certain, to make a choice, so she didn't have to.

'Hey. Don't be like that. Look, it's a confusing time. But ever since we met…' His hand reached across the duvet towards her, and his mouth cocked into its customary half-smile. The first time she'd seen it, that smile had been infuriating; now she found it tempting. But after the last couple of days – the dead woman, the fight with Noah, the endless questions about everyone's motives – she couldn't trust anybody. Nor did she want to. She sprang up off the bed.

'No. Smiles and vague remarks aren't going to cut it. This is stupid.' Audrey laughed angrily and hid her face in her hands. She knew she was being unfair. But some cruel streak in her – cruel to him or to herself, she wasn't sure – made her push on. When she looked up, she was calm. 'Thanks for the kiss, it was a nice one. But as you say, we just met.' She looked around the room slowly, taking in the piled-up detritus of a failed life chapter, the bed pushed against the wall like a student's, all the opposite of what she'd been looking for. Then her gaze returned to him. 'This isn't going anywhere.'

His eyes filled with hurt, and she regretted the last remark, but she said nothing else. She gathered her things and left, followed by the soulful eyes of the dog. When she got to the bottom of the stairs outside the flat, she opened her mouth and let out a silent scream, balling up her fists and screwing her eyes shut. What the hell was she doing? She walked away, determined to think of absolutely anything besides snakes, suicide, Kingcups and kisses.

CHAPTER 15

Of course, that was all she could think about. She stomped around the village green, fuming mostly, but for some reason leaking tears as well. It was silly to care this much. As he'd said, they barely knew each other. And if she'd been in his position, she'd probably also have been more worried about building bridges with a new family member than seeing how far things went with some random girl.

Only that kiss hadn't felt random. It had felt right.

But it couldn't be. Griffin was just some guy who still lived with his mother. He was light years away from her own life, spiritually and geographically. She'd known him for all of five minutes, during most of which she'd felt irritated by him. And however ill-defined her relationship with Noah had been, she had been dating him for months; long enough, if it was truly over, to be susceptible to a rebound. It was a stupid time to get involved with anyone, let alone someone with the many faults she'd already ascribed to Griffin. So it was good that she'd walked out. It was better this way. Her tear ducts just hadn't realised it yet.

After circling the green a couple of times, angrily brushing away tears and berating herself for her stupid taste in men, she began to register the outside world again. The villagers in their white clothes were gathered on the green once more. Many of them were staring at her, and she guessed what they were muttering. Down from London, death at the big house, disrupting our rites... But there was quite a crowd now, as the hour of the rite approached, and mixed in among the villagers were a couple of police constables, who must have been called in because of the number of revellers. Their dark uniforms reminded her of the more serious matter at hand: not whether she and Noah were broken up, but whether he would get out of jail.

She needed to talk to DI Morgan. He had to know what she now knew – or thought very likely, anyway – about Noah. Perhaps he already did; he'd bounded off on the trail of something significant when she'd last seen him. But neither she nor Griffin had actually heard what information Reverend Pascoe had given the detective. She should find Morgan and make sure.

But where to look? A glance through the pub window showed only villagers in their white clothes. She turned back to the green. Varley was in the crowd, and she approached and asked after his superior. The man scratched his jaw and looked around – it was as big a mystery to him. 'He'll be along soon enough, I'm sure. Not one to miss the serpent dance.' He stopped scanning the green and gave her a keen look. 'Was there something you needed to share with the police?'

Here was her chance, and yet she hesitated. Morgan had made no secret of his liking for her, whereas Varley had a more strictly professional air. She thought with embarrassment of his dispassionate inspection of her underwear before they'd left Trevennick House. And they were surrounded by white-garbed villagers, many of whom were staring at her. She would prefer to have this conversation in private, with a friendly face. Better if she could find Morgan. 'Nothing like that,' she replied with a false smile. 'Just wanted to ask how he left Noah.' And she walked off, hoping she'd stumble across Morgan soon, somewhere well away from all these curious looks.

She struck off into the village at random. But she couldn't shake the feeling that eyes were following her through the narrow, tilted streets, looking out from upstairs windows, noticing the foreign element. Her breath came faster and she felt herself hurrying, though she wasn't headed anywhere in particular, hurrying and looking behind, thinking someone or something would come around the corner after her, she felt it, she felt—

She bumped into someone, and gave a little shriek as they grabbed onto her. But it was only to stop them both falling.

Cameron let go and stepped away once he had righted her. 'In a rush? The ceremony's the other way, and it won't start for a while.'

'No, I… I thought… never mind. Are you all right?'

'I'm great.'

She stepped back and searched his face for hostility – his response had struck her as a little passive-aggressive, given that he was freshly bereaved and had been punched in the face today. But he was smiling, he seemed cheerful, unexpectedly friendly. Perhaps he was trying to ease the awkwardness. She returned his smile, tentatively. 'I'm sorry about all that on the green.'

'It's fine, it's fine. Honestly. Water under the bridge. I'm just reeling, I got carried away. And tensions run high around Golowan.' But he didn't seem tense, more excited. His tanned face was slightly marked by the fight, but behind the bruises and cuts his eyes were shining, hectic even. 'You can feel nature taking over, can't you?'

'Sure.' I prefer the veneer of civilisation, she thought, but he didn't seem like the right audience for this sentiment.

He had been leaning into the back of a van when she bumped into him – she saw surfboards, wetsuits, towels and food wrappers all tangled together, the detritus of his daily life. Now he turned back and reached for a bag with white fabric peeping out of it.

'Is that your outfit for the ceremony?'

'Yup. They let me take it from the big house, but I'm staying in the village now. Off to get changed. I like to spend some time in the woods to prepare.'

'Prepare?' Audrey wasn't sure what this involved – aside from the obby osses, all she'd seen people do was stand around the green, staring.

'*Connect* maybe is the better term. This land is full of spirit. The ritual works best when we remember that.' He spoke fervently. 'With everything that's happened, I need to dial in to the energy tonight. Connect to something bigger, you know?'

'I understand. You're a real nature lover.'

He smiled thinly, like he found the label demeaning. 'I try to spend most of my time outdoors.'

This tracked with the contents of his van and the square, muscular physique. Audrey could see why Stella had been attracted to him, though he seemed to be a difficult personality, always veering between strong emotions. Then again, it was natural to ricochet between feelings in grief. He carried on speaking.

'What about you? It must be good to get away from the city. Cities are like cataracts for the soul. They stop you from seeing clearly.'

She laughed, but trailed off nervously when she saw how serious he looked. 'I'm happy in London.' Though this wasn't strictly true. She continued with something that was. 'I haven't spent this much time outdoors since I was in the Girl Guides.'

'Too bad. Your cortisol levels must be off the charts. Plus concrete is the third biggest source of carbon emissions on the planet. Not a lot of people know that,' he said, nodding sagely.

Audrey actually did know that, one of the depressing statistics she'd picked up doing background research for her next book, but she thought it was better to leave Cameron feeling superior. She also decided not to ask him if he'd seen DI Morgan, and risk souring his mood by turning his mind back to the fight and to Stella's death. Let him find solace in his weirdly keen communion with nature. She said goodbye and he carried on down the hill towards the green, the river and the woods.

She walked on, unsure of where to look, and when she arrived at the church she decided to go in. Morgan probably wasn't here, but the vicar might be, and she was the one who'd last spoken to him. She might tell Audrey where he'd been headed.

The church was blessedly – yes, that was the word – cool and dim after the glare of sun outside. It was also empty of any human presence. She was no closer to finding Morgan, but it felt good to be alone, away from prying eyes. Audrey paced slowly up and down the central aisle, her breathing slowing, her heart still ruffled but her mind quietening down. She sat and leaned forward, resting her head on the wooden pew back in front of her, letting the silence and the cool penetrate her.

Audrey was so tired. All the chaos of the past twenty-four hours sat heavily on her; she wasn't sure she could move if she wanted to. A death. A break-up, maybe. A fight. A kiss, a rejection. Poor sleep. Her deadline. The hot sun, the strange atmosphere of the place. It was all too much. She needed a rest. More than that. She wanted to go home.

She didn't want to sleep, in spite of her exhaustion – she was afraid, after all that, of what she might dream. But the cool air and her great weariness pressed on her, and soon, though she struggled, she was slipping into the dark.

Audrey woke with a start and looked around, but she was still alone. She could tell by the light coming through the stained glass that some time had passed; the sun was at a low angle now. Her mouth tasted awful. She got up and stretched, trying to shake off the nap, and looked around.

It was a church in use: fresh flowers on the altar and tucked under the font, embroidered kneelers whose colours had yet to fade. She dredged up some of the art history she'd had to do for her degree to try and date the church. A wooden barrel vault and fluted stone pillars that formed pointed arches – late medieval or early modern, she guessed.

The font, currently empty of water, looked like it might be older. Winged faces formed the corners, and around the sides various animals twisted and reared against twining leaves and chains: horses, birds, serpents, rams. Or at least she could spot all the parts of those creatures. But they seemed curiously mixed and rearranged, like the obby osses for the ceremony: there were horses with beaks, and serpents with ram's heads. She knelt to look closer, drawn in by the finely chiselled curving lines which seemed to show them moving, the enigmatic angel faces, the animals that couldn't quite be placed. She nearly headbutted the stone in surprise when a voice came from behind her.

'I see you've found one of our parish treasures.'

It was Lamorna Pascoe. Audrey rose, annoyed that the woman had sneaked up on her and trying to hide her annoyance. But the vicar was flustered by having startled her and flapped about, apologising.

'Oh dear, that was a near miss. I'm so used to the parquet, you see – I've become accustomed to stepping over the squeaky bits.'

'It's a beautiful font,' said Audrey, trying to move on.

'Norman. Twelfth century, it's believed.'

'The rest of the church is newer, isn't it? It almost seems to have been built around the font.'

The vicar nodded enthusiastically. 'Doesn't it? Of course, I'm sure that wouldn't have been practical, but this font… You usually think of the altar as the heart of a church, but here the font is the centre of things, the source. As though people have been worshipping round it forever.'

Audrey looked again at the grey stone, the twisting shapes, the unreadable angels. 'Curious animals, all jumbled up together.'

The other woman stepped around her to get closer to the font, and reached out a hand to trace one of the ram-headed serpents. Her blush still hadn't subsided, and her eyes were shining with heightened emotion. 'People worshipped animals long before the church got here, combining their most powerful attributes, granting their characteristics to gods and vice versa. Locals were praying to ram-headed serpents and beaked horses and those other-world agents, the birds, a thousand years before this carving was thought of.'

'You don't seem to feel any professional rivalry.'

The vicar straightened and gave her a surprisingly condescending smile for a woman who always seemed to be recovering from some minor upset. 'It's my belief that the sacred is eternal. It's how we show our reverence that changes over time.'

Audrey made a noncommittal noise. She wasn't at all in the right frame of mind to discuss the evolution of religion with an actual priest. Then she remembered why she'd come. 'You don't know where DI Morgan is, do you?'

The vicar looked at her searchingly. 'Haven't seen him. But he'll be at the river once the rite begins. What did you need him for?'

Once again, Audrey hesitated. People told priests their secrets, but somehow she didn't like to confide in Lamorna. The woman was always either getting in a flap or saying something vaguely Druidical. It didn't inspire confidence. And anyway, what could she do about Noah's situation? 'Just wanted a chat,' she said finally, hoping this would pass unchallenged. 'He's been very helpful in this whole situation.' She turned away, looking around the church for something else to comment on, or even better, for some excuse to leave. But then the vicar came out with something wholly unexpected.

'Is it one of the Kingcup boys? Is that why you're upset?'

Audrey was so taken aback that she didn't bother to deny this. 'How did you know?'

'As a fellow sufferer, I recognise the signs.'

There was a first, anxious stab of thought: not Griffin? But then Audrey remembered the first time she'd seen the Reverend Pascoe, and who with. A more likely and less perturbing possibility presented itself. 'Trevor?'

The vicar nodded, a curious expression on her face: a kind of martyrdom around the eyes, mixed with pleasure about the mouth.

Audrey wondered if this was the first time she'd told anyone, and then wondered why she'd told her.

'Not an easy man to love. Be grateful you've fallen for the brother with the sunny disposition.' So it was Pascoe who needed a confidante. It must be hard, as a priest, when you were the one with a secret to share. Perhaps speaking to an outsider was safer for her. Audrey tried to picture the two of them together, cosily chatting about the Kingcup brothers and their maddening ways over a glass of wine, like sisters-in-law in a sitcom. The dog collar struck an odd note.

'I wouldn't exactly say I've fallen for him. We only met a day ago.'

'And you were part of a couple. Move on fast, don't you?'

Audrey felt suddenly on guard, thrown by the insult – or had it only been tactlessness, the vicar's habit of stepping one toe across the line? Her senses were pricked, and she was aware of everything around them: the mixed scents of flowery sweetness, stone dust and warm wood in the air; the light through the stained glass shifting as a cloud cleared away from the sun; the position Reverend Pascoe occupied, between her and the door.

The woman's head was cocked queryingly, an encouraging smile on her face, as though waiting for Audrey to confide. As though she hadn't just called her a slut, in however round-about a way. Audrey thought of a snake grinning at its prey, the smile getting wider and wider, until – snap!

'Better to move fast than not move at all.'

She hadn't been sure of her target, but the vicar's flinch let her know she'd chosen correctly. The dishwasher full of several days' worth of mismatched mugs; the way she and Trevor had been arguing – she was a middle-aged woman with a crush, not someone in a relationship. Audrey braced for the next round, but the other woman just straightened her cocked head and smiled as though nothing awkward had passed, saying, 'Speaking of getting going, we'd better head for the river.'

She held out an ushering arm, and Audrey passed in front of her out of the church.

'You've come all this way, it would be such a shame to miss this part of the ritual. We call it the serpent dance.'

CHAPTER 16

It was midsummer; the days were long. The light was fading, but the sun was still hot, and would be slanting golden for hours yet, across the village, the green, the river and the high tops of the woods.

Out of the houses and through the narrow streets came a trickle of villagers, each trickle uniting with the next until there was a great swell of them, flowing towards the river. At first Audrey walked with the vicar, but soon she lost her in the crowd, though it should have been easy to spot her priestly black. Most of the villagers were wearing white: shirts, trousers, dresses, with the only colour the embroidered blue sash, tied around the waist or diagonally over the chest. She saw Morwenna, still in her blue-and-white striped T-shirt but now wearing the kind of flowing skirt Audrey had imagined she'd usually affect, long and white, rippling around her legs as she walked at a stately pace among the others.

DI Morgan, too, was there. She recognised the back of his unseasonable tweed jacket and wondered if he'd dropped police business to attend. Then, as the current of the procession turned with the street, she saw him from the side. He was wearing a ram's skull which completely obscured his face. She shuddered and remembered that he had been a local before he became a policeman.

No church bell had rung, no signal had been given, but the people knew their hour. A human tide flowed towards the green, silent mostly, though here and there a few would break out into snatches of song. Audrey expected them to halt at the green with its circle of obby osses and the prepared bonfire, but instead the crowd split around the sculptures, reuniting on the other side, by the riverbank. Then the flow of people turned and walked upriver, away from the green and the village. They didn't go far, only a quarter of a mile or so, the distance required to be out of sight of the houses; but with so many moving together, progress was slow.

They stopped at a place where the bank sloped down at a shallow angle and broadened into a small pebbly beach. It did the same on the opposite side, slowing the river's pace and making a ford you could cross into the woods. The clusters of singers had slowly joined together, and now the whole crowd was giving voice to a looping refrain whose Cornish words Audrey couldn't make sense of. *Dhe'n gwer yn hans kerthys'vy… Ow quary dro tansys.* What had begun as song shifted closer to chant as more voices joined.

Now Lamorna appeared again, the first to wade into the river, lifting a small withy figure – an animal, but on a tiny scale, unlike the ones on the green – high above her head, then bending to place it on the water, where the current drew it down and away. Next came DI Morgan in his skull mask, splashing into the deeper water below the ford. Audrey saw now that he wasn't the only one so adorned: other villagers wore ram's heads, and one had hidden his face in a huge horse's skull and was wrapped in a large black cloak from which emerged two sticks, which he used like crutches. Under the weight of the skull, he moved like a skeleton, broken and frightening.

Morwenna, too, waded into the river, and the man who'd tutted over Cameron after the fight: the prominent citizens of the village, leading the way. Each gave the river a little figure of grass and sticks, and then they turned and mounted the bank again as others lined up to take their place. All the while the song went on, lilting and droning. Audrey was unsettled, as she had been since arriving here, but now she was also mesmerised, as though the music were beating through her blood. She felt tempted, almost, to look into the shadows on the opposite bank.

The file of white-clad figures entered the water, lifted and released their offerings, waded out and began to walk back down the riverbank to the village. Soon there was a crowd of them retracing their steps, and she'd lost sight of those who had first made their offering to the river.

Audrey stood there with the villagers – worshippers, now – flowing around her like she was one of the rocks in the river. She still had her bag over her shoulder, and she found herself reaching for her sketchbook. Opening it, she began to draw, working quickly, taking down fast sketches of the figures in the river: a man lifting his offering, a woman's long skirt streaming water as she climbed back up the bank.

She wanted to capture the feeling of the ritual, the way the song produced a kind of trance, the way the evening light made everyone glow. Her pencil moved with assurance; for the first time in a long while she felt her brain getting out of the way, no self-doubt or embarrassment about her work to interrupt the link between eye and hand. Later it would occur to her that perhaps it was a violation to document a sacred rite, but now it felt like she was a participant, like she, too, had a preordained role in the pattern, one she must play if everything were to unfold as it should.

In and out of the river flowed the villagers, and back down the bank; on flowed the song. Although every action was carried out with reverential slowness, soon there were only a few waiting to make their offering, and the sound of the song was strongest further away. Audrey could see now why it was called the serpent dance – an endless twining, set to music. And the chant was calling her on, it was larger than her, frightening but impossible to deny. She began to move with the last of the crowd, back towards the green, stopping for a minute here or there to take down a few lines of what she saw. Girls in a row with their blue sashes; the dark, tree-sheltered mouth of the tributary where Griffin had taken her, feeding into the river and hastening its movement; the small animals, twisted out of stems and flowers, bobbing on the current or drowning.

She almost didn't notice when she bumped into the Kingcup brothers. Trevor didn't seem to see her. He was singing full-throatedly and gazing at the water, barely looking where he was going. His white and blue garments, wet to the waist and clinging, showed he'd waded in further than most. Audrey thought of the passion with which he'd spoken of the river. She could understand it better now she'd seen what she'd seen – the river did seem to make its own demands.

Griffin definitely did notice her; his eyes flicked towards her and then away more than once. She tried not to meet his gaze. She tried, too, not to think of what this strange and beautiful occasion might have been like if she'd been watching it by his side, sharing complicit looks, perhaps wading into the water together. She wouldn't have been a mere stone parting the current then; she could have been a part of the flow. Instead, she pushed past him, intensely aware of the air between them, charged with anger and hurt.

The encounter had broken her mood of rapt observation, and she couldn't seem to lose herself again in the otherworldly atmosphere. She trudged along among those still caught up in the ritual, feeling sorry for herself, and a bit silly. It was stupid to be this upset about a man she'd only met the other day. But it would have been nice to share the occasion with somebody. With anybody. Even Noah, as much as things had gone wrong between them.

Her pity changed direction, turning outward to Noah. He was stuck in a holding cell while this was happening, when it had been his idea to come and see the ritual in the first place. Strange, how much less furious she felt at Noah than she did at Griffin, even though they'd known each other for longer, shared a bed. But they hadn't shared much else, had they? She'd so often felt alone when they were together.

And now she really was alone in this crowd. They were back at the village green and the bridge, everyone gathering together. She looked around, trying to spot the people she'd met since coming here, carefully avoiding looking in Griffin's direction. There was Cameron, arms crossed, standing on the bank and gazing at the river. There was the vicar, stood on the bridge, also looking into the water. Morwenna was nearby; Audrey wouldn't mind exchanging a word and a smile with her, but it probably wasn't a good idea, given what had happened with her son. Maybe DI Morgan was still around – the ram's skull was a bit disturbing, but he'd always been kind. She felt he was on her side.

There was a stir and pullulation around the bridge, presumably the next stage of the ritual. Audrey tried to edge closer to see what form it would take. But as she pressed through the crowd she noted a change in the atmosphere. The singing had stopped, and people were looking at each other, worried, speaking in low voices. There was a broken feeling in the air.

When she got to the front of the crowd, she saw a body in the water.

CHAPTER 17

The body was that of a man, tall and solid, caught against the pillars of the bridge, the cold water flowing in a smooth arc over his front. His eyes were open, gazing at but not seeing the sky; though his face was clearly visible, Audrey recognised him by his jacket before she could take in his features. It was DI Morgan. 'He's lost his ram's skull,' she said, to nobody in particular. There wasn't anyone to listen to her anyway; the villagers were knotted together, murmuring dismay, hands over mouths, arms around each other to offer comfort at this further loss of one of their own.

Eventually a couple of men waded into the water and pulled the body to shore. The water was deeper here; soon it would join the main flow to the estuary. It was hard work, fighting against the current, and they were wet to their necks by the time they had wrangled the stiff corpse onto the bank. They collapsed in the grass, breathing heavily, the rise and fall of their chests in active contrast to the still body next to them.

As the policeman had been dragged out of the water and the back of his head exposed, a gasp had gone up. The skull was broken – blood and something pinker leaked from a narrow crack in the bone. A first explanation was offered, by one of the blue-sashed locals: 'He must have fallen and hit his head.'

'The river must have its due,' said someone else. Audrey shivered and wished they weren't all in the same clothes; it was difficult to tell them apart.

'He was alive just a few minutes ago,' said yet another blue sash.

She tried to think how long it had been – it was hard to judge time in the trance-like state the singing and the ritual gestures had induced. But surely it could have taken no more than twenty minutes for the villagers to make their offerings and travel the short distance back downriver to the bridge?

'Didn't anyone see him go down? Lamorna, you were in the river with him right at the start.' This was Trevor, standing on the bank, calling up to the vicar on the bridge.

She stuttered a reply. 'I – I wish I had. I stopped to watch those coming up from behind, I thought he'd just gone further ahead of me on the path.'

People had fallen silent to listen to this exchange, but now a general murmur started up again as Varley pushed through the crowd and waved them back from the body. He circled the dead man slowly a couple of times, taking stock. He shook his head and squeezed his eyes tight shut, and Audrey remembered that, like many here, he'd known Morgan; determining what had happened wasn't simply a job to be done. Varley sank down onto his haunches and gingerly adjusted the head so he could see the wound better. Or tried to – the body was stiff and resisted his examination, just as it had resisted being pulled from the water. He frowned and turned to the men who had done the pulling to ask them a quiet question.

Everyone else began speculating and lamenting among themselves. Audrey had no one to speak to – everyone here was either a stranger to her or to be avoided for one reason or another. She couldn't help looking at Griffin, and this time they didn't manage to avoid each other's eyes; but his hurt gaze broke away. She tried to quell self-pity. Her tender feelings should be for DI Morgan. A good man was dead.

It was strange that no one had seen him go down. Audrey tried to calculate the distance between the ford and the bridge. A quarter of a mile? Not much further than that, certainly. And the water was only deep enough to carry a body along for part of that stretch. There had been people trailing along the river close to him the entire time. It seemed impossible that no one had noticed the fall, the splash, a struggle, his dark form caught in the current.

Audrey pushed closer to the body. The eyes were still open, but empty and a little clouded. River water, dark with silt, trickled from his sleeves and mouth. Wet hair was plastered across his pale forehead. He'd been a sizeable man, a large, bluff presence, but now his very size made his corpse the more vulnerable. He looked… felled. She thought of his gentle, reassuring manner towards her, which had been a little courtly, gallant even. She thought, too, of the few things he'd told her about himself: his years working in different cities, this last post near home before retirement, the hints of loneliness and a private life unfulfilled. He'd never get a chance now to find love, to fill his life's last chapter with something good. All because of a stupid slippery river rock, a silly accident.

Her sketchbook was already in her hand, and Audrey started to draw the man stretched on the grass – the second dead body she'd had occasion to sketch in the space of two days. There was a loose thread somewhere in her mind, but she couldn't find it to give it a pull.

A hand slapped down over her drawing and an angry voice said, 'What are you doing?' She looked up. Trevor was standing opposite her, anger in his face.

'I just wanted to – it's what I do, I didn't mean any disrespect.'

'But you've given it. Let me see that.' Before she could react, he yanked the sketchbook from her hands and began flipping through it.

Griffin stepped forward and reached out a restraining hand towards his brother, though he didn't look at Audrey. 'Trev—'

'Look at this. And the other stuff she's been drawing.' Trevor held up a page with Stella's bloodied throat on it, thrusting it in Audrey's face and then showing it round. Most of the villagers were watching now, though their reactions were as yet undecided, attention torn between the body freshly pulled from the river and the new disturbance.

'Is that my Stella? Did she draw her dead?' said Cameron, stepping forward from the crowd. He was soaked up to the chest; he must have been one of the men to draw DI Morgan from the water.

'And you, too.' Trevor turned the pages carelessly, creasing them and making a small tear with his hasty hands. He showed Cameron his own bloodied face, drawn after the fight with Noah. It wasn't a flattering image – he looked like a sullen schoolboy who'd been bested on the playground.

The living face turned to her wearing an angry snarl. 'What the fuck is wrong with you? That's sick, that is. You're sick!'

'No! Please, give it back.' Audrey reached ineffectually for the book, looking round at the growing circle of hostile faces, trying to explain. 'It's just what I do – it helps make sense of things. I didn't mean anything by it, they're only for me.'

Trevor had continued his rough handling of her sketches and now found another page that arrested his attention. This time there was no person depicted, no blood or any other noticeably private thing, only a jumble of small objects.

'What are these?' He held the page up to her and glared.

'It's just some stuff I saw on Stella's dresser. Mussel shells and pebbles, little things she kept. They caught my eye…' She trailed off lamely, looking around for support, though without much hope. But it came as Griffin stepped in again.

'Give it back. She hasn't done any harm.' He still wouldn't meet her eyes. Trevor's gaze was fixed on the drawing, and he seemed not to notice his brother's tug on his arm. Griffin peered into the bent face. 'Trev?'

'Have it, then.' Trevor threw the book down on the grass at her feet, torn and wet. Audrey stooped to pick it up, and kept her head down, leafing through the pages to assess the damage, afraid to look around and see an entire village watching her. Her heart was beating quickly and her face was hot. It was horrible, embarrassing, but why did she feel so afraid? Was there some worse threat than this public shaming before strangers, something darker lurking in the thick, tense air? And why had she seen a flash of fear in Trevor's eyes too?

But attention was pulled back to the cluster around Morgan as Varley, who'd been speaking in hushed tones with the men who had taken him from the river, burst out, 'He's been dead for hours!'

A general silence fell. The village was small, but there were still a few hundred souls gathered on the riverbank; coughing and shuffling and whispered remarks meant that even the most respectful silence wasn't quite silent. Now it was truly quiet, as everyone struggled to comprehend what the policeman had said. There was only the rush of the river, the murmuring birds – and then the strain of understanding broke, and people began voicing their questions and objections.

'What do you mean?'

'Impossible.'

'You must be confused – we all saw him making his offering to the river less than an hour ago.'

'Never mind, never mind,' said Varley. He had the nervous, embarrassed look of a schoolboy caught playing truant; he must have let the remark slip without meaning to, disarmed by shock and grief. But he had let it slip, and now the villagers were pressing closer, a questioning crowd that wouldn't be denied. Varley gave in and held up his hand, and the competing voices subsided. 'Rigor mortis has set in. This man can't have been dead for less than four hours. And that's all I'm going to say, so leave it.'

The murmurs swelled, and again an objection came. This time Audrey recognised the speaker. It was Cameron, still dripping silty river water into the grass. 'That can't be. We were all up at the ford, and we all saw Morgan wade into the river and then start walking back. It's barely half an hour since then.'

The policeman listened, stood, and looked down at the body. He didn't scratch the back of his head, but Audrey was sure he wanted to. 'So you're telling me that a man who was alive less than an hour ago has managed to seize up like someone dead four or five hours? How do you figure that?'

'I'm no doctor,' responded Cameron. 'But the water's cold, could that explain it?'

Audrey felt a bit sorry for him, thrust into the role of village spokesperson, trying to make sense of the baffling situation. But there was little sense to be made.

'If he was cold, then rigor would have taken longer to set in.' Varley closed his mouth with finality and refused further attempts to draw him on the subject. The village remained in perplexity, waiting for the ambulance to arrive. Quiet, frightened conversations went on in small groups. Theories were developed and discarded, but everyone was struck by the occurrence of a second tragic death in two days. Audrey kept hearing the words *river* and *tithe*.

She wondered if Lamorna would say something. Surely, as priest of the parish, it was her job to provide reassurance, to make sense of the stunning fact of death. But she looked as disturbed as anyone, standing stone-still on the bridge, her hands gripping the parapet, her eyes fixed on the dead body below. Occasionally she wrenched them away to look at Trevor, but they were always drawn back.

Varley, too, gazed fixedly at the body he was guarding. His legs were firmly planted a little wider than his hips, his arms crossed in front of his chest, a stance that said he would not be moved. The only thing that did move was an angry little muscle in his jaw.

Morwenna, Trevor and Griffin were all immersed in conversations with their neighbours. Audrey felt self-conscious, a disconnected presence bearing witness to a local tragedy. Self-conscious and therefore vulnerable. But she wasn't the only one. Cameron, like herself, was standing apart, though people cast anxious little glances his way. Perhaps he was isolated by his recent loss, and it seemed frivolous to involve him in speculation about this new death.

Nervously waiting along with everyone, Audrey turned back to her notebook, trying to smooth the pages rumpled by Trevor's rude inspection. There were some creases that wouldn't come out, and some charcoal lines smudged by water or rough handling, but the drawings had mostly survived. There were her fresh sketches of the villagers at the river, DI Morgan among them in his ram's skull and tweed jacket, and, flipping back, innocent drawings of people and houses and flowers, along with the more disturbing ones of Stella, which had been judged so offensive. There was DI Morgan again, standing over the corpse with a sad face and—

Audrey stopped rifling through the images.

It wasn't a photograph. It wasn't exact. It wasn't anything you could call evidence. But however uncertain of her vision and worth as an artist Audrey felt, she was confident of her skills as a draughtsperson.

And the DI Morgan she'd drawn here had a different set to his shoulders than the one in the ram's skull she'd seen by the river. As recorded by her pencil, his posture and weight and bearing didn't match.

He was wearing the same jacket. But it wasn't the same man.

CHAPTER 18

Where to take this knowledge? After what had happened with Griffin, Audrey had no ally in the village. She was an outsider who'd made a frightening discovery, relying on the same intrusive sketches that had angered everyone moments ago.

Another frightening realisation followed quickly on the first. Someone had been impersonating DI Morgan during the ritual. And that someone presumably had a deadly reason to resent being exposed. Unless the river really did have magical properties, there was the far more concretely frightening prospect of a murderer in their midst. If she told the wrong person…

It was impossible, though, to feel that any man would be an equally dangerous confidant. However irrevocable their argument, Griffin wasn't involved in anything nefarious. His brother, though – his brooding looks and angry words made that easier to believe. And there'd been something in his face, something to do with her drawings, that made her sure he was bound up in all this. But if he was involved, could his brother be innocent?

Or perhaps none of them were. The whole village had felt like the site of a conspiracy since she arrived. Tight-knit, fierce about its traditions, seemingly cut off from the rest of the world. Who knows what madness they might all join in for the sake of appeasing the river one year more?

Varley, though, by virtue of working for the police, was at least a semi-outsider. He was the most obvious person for her to tell. His allegiance, she hoped, was to law and order, not to local custom. Whether he would listen to her, a woman he'd first encountered at another death scene, was something she'd just have to find out.

Audrey approached the man, though he was so concentrated on the corpse before him that it was difficult to catch his eye without stepping disrespectfully close to the body. 'Er – Sergeant Varley, wasn't it?' He raised his eyebrows, waiting for her to explain her approach. 'Can I show you something?'

He made no gesture of invitation, but continued to look at her, his posture unchanged, still standing guard over his fallen colleague.

'This might seem odd, or like nothing, but… do you see the drawing I did of DI Morgan, here?'

Varley looked briefly at the page, then flicked his eyes back to her face, waiting.

'That was him earlier, at the river. You can't see his face, because of the ram's skull, but that's his jacket, and we all assumed it was him. But if you look at this drawing of him from the night Stella Penrose died…' She flipped the pages to find the drawing she'd seen, hurried, gabbling and unsure of what the expressionless Varley was thinking. 'Here. You see how he stands, the set of the shoulders, less weight around the middle? It might be the same jacket, but it's not the same man.'

Varley leaned forward a little to give the drawing a closer look. Then he righted himself and scratched his temple with a thoughtful finger. Finally, for the first time since she'd approached him, he spoke. 'Let me get this straight. You drew Morgan on the night of Stella Penrose's suicide, for some reason—'

'I didn't mean any disrespect,' said Audrey quickly, stomach sinking. This line hadn't worked well earlier. 'But if you remember, I'm a professional artist. It's a kind of way of making sense of what's happening. Some people have a journal. Or a drink.'

'Is that a joke? It's hardly the time.'

This wasn't going well. Audrey pressed on, but with less and less hope of being understood. 'Of course not. I'm just trying to explain why I do this. The point is, it's a reflex, and, without wanting to sound arrogant, I'm good at it. My drawings are pretty accurate.'

This was perhaps the most confident she'd ever sounded in her skills, and inwardly she smiled at the irony – it wasn't success but a series of unexplained deaths that had finally got her to assert her own talent. Varley didn't have the same faith in her skill, though.

'I'm sure they are. Regardless, miss, they're only drawings. Even a pair of photographs where the man's build looks different wouldn't be proof of much without the face.

And a drawing? Not worth the paper, as far as the law's concerned.'

'But don't you see something's off here? You said yourself he shouldn't be this stiff if he only went into the water a little while ago. This shows it wasn't him who went in.'

'And all these people,' said Varley, gesturing at the assembled villagers, 'who've known him his whole life, lived next to him, you think they wouldn't recognise the man? And you would?' His tone was souring, and he spoke a little louder now. Their exchange had started to attract attention, and the first person to approach was Trevor. Audrey's heartbeat quickened; her attempt to explain was already going badly, and she was sure he would make it worse.

'What's she showing you there?'

'Mr Kingcup, you don't need to get involved. This is police business and I'll handle it myself.'

At least Varley's sense of professionalism prevented him from offering her as a scapegoat to the village. But Trevor wasn't going to be deterred.

'Is it the pictures of the dead woman, and the things in her room? It's obscene. Intruding in a death like that. She'll be drawing Paul here, regardless of how those of us who knew him feel. Give her two seconds and she'll be drawing him.'

Audrey looked around, hoping Griffin would step forward again. He was close, watching his brother, but he wouldn't meet her eyes. A cold trickle of disappointment went through her. What had she expected? He'd already made clear that his loyalty lay with his family. The rest of the villagers, too, were looking at her with a hostile blankness that made her shudder, massed as they all were in front of their wicker statues, wearing their identical outfits. They could easily turn as one against her. She was frightened, and yet some stubborn instinct pushed her to defend herself.

'Anyway, why do you care so much?' she challenged Trevor, before Varley could make another calming, official remark. 'What bothers you about my drawings? You seem very involved. Who was wearing DI Morgan's jacket an hour ago?'

Trevor stepped closer to her, his face and posture threatening. 'If there's anything fishy here, the stink is coming from you. Probably covering for your idiot city boyfriend.'

'Oh, I'm the fishy one? And yet you're the fisherman. With your mussel ropes, and your weird obsession with the river.'

She didn't think this was the sharpest comeback, but the blood had drained from his face and he'd fallen back. Whatever she'd said had hit a nerve – the same nerve that her drawings had. Her drawing of mussel shells—

'Here, that's enough,' Varley was saying, and was making herding gestures with his hands to try and shoo them away without leaving his post. 'Have some respect, the both of you. There's a dead man here, he doesn't need you arguing over his corpse.'

Trevor was pulled away by his mother and brother. The Reverend Pascoe had approached during their argument. She put a hand on Audrey's shoulder now and said, 'Come back to the vicarage. You won't be able to catch a train home this evening either.'

The past couple of hours had almost made Audrey forget that she had her own life, her own problems outside of this place. This morning she had been so irritated to be stuck here another day, and now here she was, involving herself, trying to sort out local mysteries. She turned to Varley. 'Can I leave in the morning?'

'Better that you do, the way you're stirring things up. As far as I can tell, there's been an accident and a suicide. We have your number. We'll contact you in London if you're needed.'

Part of her wasn't ready to give up. She wanted to bring up the rigor mortis, the odd angle of Stella's knife wound. But Varley was right. Better leave the explanations where they were, firmly anchored in the obvious facts; better not to get more deeply involved.

She nodded goodbye and he returned the gesture, evidently relieved to be rid of her. Lamorna drew her off, and they headed for the vicarage, crossing the green in the last of the golden midsummer light. Audrey was glad, in the circumstances, to be getting in before dark.

CHAPTER 19

At the vicarage, Audrey collapsed into a kitchen chair. Lamorna said nothing, just moved quietly from sink to stove, preparing a meal. Soon there was a smell of onions in hot oil, and Audrey realised she was starving. She felt the weakness of hunger, intensified by the weakness of gratitude. It was another kaleidoscopic turn of her feelings. A couple of hours ago, in the church, she'd been disturbed by Lamorna, almost threatened, and now, after what had happened by the river, she felt a childlike sense of relief that there was someone older and more responsible who could take charge of her needs. The whole weekend had been full of such reversals, trust and liking broken, formed again, and broken again too quickly. 'Thank you,' she said.

'You haven't tasted it yet,' replied Lamorna with a smile. 'Bachelor cooking is about all I can manage, I'm afraid. I always burn the onions.'

'I meant for – well, for everything. Getting me out of there, I guess.'

'It's a tight-knit community. They were always going to

turn on outsiders when harm kept coming to their own. But you weren't in any real danger.'

Audrey didn't find this as reassuring as Lamorna seemed to intend. She hadn't thought she was in danger. Or at least she hadn't wanted to give the thought credence. But at least she was safe now.

She sat at the table while Lamorna carried on cooking, turning the pages of her sketchbook, brooding on her failure to make herself understood. She was an outsider, it was true, and there was no particular reason they should trust or listen to her.

No particular reason except that she was right. She couldn't explain everything that had occurred, but someone had been at that riverbank pretending to be DI Morgan. Which meant he really had been dead for as long as the rigor mortis indicated, and that someone didn't want that known. And there was only one reason they wouldn't.

Murder.

She shivered in spite of the warm weather and the hot stove. Suddenly everything she looked at had a sordid, yellowish cast. She'd felt something awful lurking in this village from the moment she arrived at the station: the looming woods, the villagers in their uniform white and blue, the snakes writhing across the church font. And now she knew she'd been right, there was something dark under all of it, even if she wasn't sure of the source of that darkness. Human evil was the most rational explanation. But way out here, among the villagers and their rituals, she found it strangely easy to believe in a river god hungry for tribute. Especially as Morgan's death wasn't easily explicable. Who better than a god to perform an impossible murder?

But there was another link in the chain, wasn't there? If DI Morgan had been murdered, only a day after Stella Penrose died, then wasn't there a good chance his suspicions had been right, and her death was wrongful too? After all, the most obvious reason to kill a detective was because he was about to uncover the truth.

She now felt sure both deaths involved foul play, but she hadn't a clue who was behind them. Two faces materialised in her mind: Noah's and Trevor's. But Noah had wanted to know Stella, not to kill her, unless he'd been a much better actor than she credited him for. And Trevor had been in full view during the river ritual; she was almost certain he couldn't have been impersonating Morgan. Noah, meanwhile, was in a holding cell and definitely hadn't been at the river. Besides, though both had strong feelings towards Stella, why would either have wanted to kill DI Morgan, a mild and friendly man?

Mild and friendly, but also a police detective. If he'd been getting close to the truth, they'd have wanted him out of the way. She remembered what he'd said to her before he rushed away from the pub the last time she'd seen him – 'I think I know how to get him out of this.' So not Noah, but someone who wanted suspicion to stay on Noah.

She tried to think how people had acted towards them since they arrived. There was obvious bad blood between Noah and Cameron, after that fight on the green. But Cameron had been out of town when the first death occurred. Trevor, too, had been hostile from the start. He'd been in full view during the ritual, though, and he wasn't any better equipped than anyone to sneak in and out of a locked glass room whose window looked over a cliff.

It all went in circles. Audrey didn't have the detecting skills or the intimate knowledge of the players she would need to piece it together. She could only see that something was wrong. She'd tried to tell them, but they wouldn't listen. At least she'd spoken up. It was more than anyone had ever done for her when she was a frightened child in an unhappy household. Fine. Let them sort out their mess themselves. The police would get to the bottom of it. Or they wouldn't. Either way, she was leaving.

Lamorna put down a plate of spaghetti and tomato sauce in front of her. In the end, she had burned the onions a little, but Audrey still fell on the food, ravenous. Her companion was less eager, and poked at her dinner with a fork, moving it around but not eating it.

'In a way, I should be thanking you,' she said.

Audrey looked up, confused, forking an undignified tangle of pasta into her mouth. Lamorna seemed bashful, eager yet reluctant; though she was speaking to Audrey, her attention was directed inward.

'What do you mean?' Audrey asked.

'It's funny – we're quite insular really. Quite self-sufficient. We forget that outsiders bring a breath of fresh air, as well as disruptions. I forget, and I used to be one.'

'You didn't grow up here, then?' asked Audrey. She'd wondered about this before. The vicar's name was Cornish enough, and she seemed very much at the heart of things in the village, but her accent was pure Home Counties.

'My father's family were from the area, but no. I grew up around Oxford. I always felt a pull, though. Dad infected me with his nostalgia. Cornwall seemed like a magical place. So, when my work brought me, I was happy. I've done all I can to make it a home.'

Audrey nodded and turned back to her food. Hunger was pressing on her attention more urgently than curiosity.

'If you hadn't come,' Lamorna carried on in a somewhat dreamy tone, 'or if your boyfriend hadn't, anyway, certain things might never have come to a head.'

'Come to a head how?' Audrey asked, unsure she wanted to hear the answer. She'd carefully reasoned through why Noah couldn't be a killer, but now it sounded like Lamorna wanted to assign him some level of blame. They might not be a couple any more, but it still gave Audrey a twinge when someone implied he was a bad person.

'Oh, I'm talking nonsense!' Lamorna seemed to come to, and waved a dismissive hand. 'The village has had a bit of a shake, and now I'm feeling... hopeful.' She got up and began to clear her plate and cutlery, though she'd eaten little. She was humming something to herself, something which made Audrey shiver. After a few bars she realised why. It was the river song.

Now the ease she'd initially felt away from the crowd, with the prospect of having her hunger sated, was thoroughly dissolved in the jaundiced anxiety that had overtaken her so many times in the past days. Lamorna was in a gentle mood, obviously well disposed towards her. This wasn't the fearful oddity she'd experienced in the church. But the other woman still unsettled her, and there was something coming into focus, something she didn't want to see.

The song. The passion people felt for the river. The locked glass bedroom, looking out over the water.

The condom in the bin. The mussel shells on the bureau. Lamorna's hopefulness.

Trevor's face when he saw her sketch.

But he hated her. And yet. Audrey was suddenly sure of it. It was Trevor. Stella had been sleeping with Trevor. And Lamorna knew about it. It was Trevor who had been in Stella's bed between Cameron's departure and her own and Noah's arrival. It was twisted, but he'd hardly be the first person in the world to find love – or at least desire – chasing after hate, a serpent eating its own tail.

Audrey tried to picture it, and found it was easier than she'd thought. Trevor was handsome, it was true, and Stella too had a lot of physical charisma; Noah hadn't wanted that from her, but Audrey had seen him fall under her spell. A bit of fame, a bit of beauty, a lot of brio. It would have given Stella pleasure to have another young lover on her string as she prepared to marry Cameron. She could see that. And it would have given Trevor pleasure to dominate the woman who'd destroyed his family; to be the one having an affair rather than part of its fallout. And, probably, though she found Freud absurd and had quickly aborted her own foray into therapy years ago, this really was a case where the Oedipus complex applied – he'd had the same woman as his absent father. She shuddered. Plenty of motivation for sex; none for affection. She wondered if those kinds of itches ever benefited from being scratched. Or did scratching them lead to murder?

But that still left the problem of how. Both murders seemed impossible. And Trevor was so obvious a person, always mouthing off and glaring at everyone. He wasn't hiding in plain sight. He wasn't hiding at all. If an outsider like her could figure out there was something between him and Stella, it would already be the talk of the village. Talk Cameron might have overheard. Jealousy had been a motive for murder before.

Then there was Lamorna, loving Trevor from afar. Another jealous heart. What itch was she scratching, a grown woman cultivating an unrequited passion, a woman whose love object was obviously damaged? But then Audrey remembered she was a priest; there was probably a saviour complex lurking there somewhere. Still, the whole thing seemed a little delusional. Just because Stella was out of the way didn't mean Trevor would come rushing into her arms.

Audrey's appetite was gone. She pushed her plate across the table and considered the vicar as she finished clearing supper, still humming to herself, still hopeful. Maybe she was right to be so; although Lamorna had none of Stella's sensual confidence or practised charm, and the ecclesiastical get-up wasn't as flattering as the curve-hugging ensembles Stella had worn, they were both buxom blonde women of a certain age – perhaps Trevor would find solace in her bed.

On the other hand, maybe there was no evil here, just a woman who'd killed herself on meeting the son she'd given away, a man who'd slipped in the river and gone stiff, a few tangled love stories. Human mess, but not dark intent. Humans were messy. It was no wonder there was the odd detail that didn't fit.

Audrey was too tired to search further for explanations, or to spend any more energy analysing the disturbing evidence of her sketches. She would be on a train in the morning, leaving all this mess behind, watching the countryside spool back up around her, rivers and hills and sheep and fields, until she was back in London and had only her own problems to worry about.

'Thanks again,' she said to her hostess. 'I didn't even help you clear the plates.' She found the vicar of Trevennick an odd, uncomfortable, at times even a disturbing presence, but she couldn't deny she'd been very generous to her. With a last burst of gratitude born of exhaustion and the knowledge there was a bed waiting for her upstairs, provided by this woman, she said, 'I hope everything works out with Trevor.'

'It must.' The eyes continued to shine. 'I've done so much for him.'

'What have you done for him?' Audrey asked with a last dart of misgiving. Lamorna clearly relished the prospect of stepping into a dead woman's shoes. Had she made sure that they would be empty?

But the vicar's response was innocent enough. 'You should see my hands at mussel harvest time,' she laughed.

Audrey nodded, smiled, and went upstairs to take her deep and dreamless rest. She was so tired she didn't even remember to be frightened of the dark.

THE FEAST OF
ST JOHN

CHAPTER 20

Audrey woke, and for the first time all weekend, the sunshine felt appropriate. Lamorna had offered to drive her to the station to catch a train after the morning service finished. She was leaving; she was going home. Perhaps it wasn't much of a home, but the problems waiting there were simpler, and the nights were better lit than in this place. She flung her things into her bag anyhow – sweater, jeans, the pointless silk nightdress, the sketchbook whose revelations had been unwanted.

Passing down the stairs, she saw Noah's bag through the half-open door of the room he'd slept in. She was surprised his things hadn't made it to the police station with him, and wondered whether she ought to take them. Perhaps he'd collect them from her in London. She tried to imagine that conversation, the different directions it could lead – towards recrimination or reconciliation. Thinking of the latter possibility, she felt a twinge of guilt, leaving him caught up in this mess and under a cloud of suspicion. She listened for sounds of the vicar moving about the house, but then she remembered she'd be conducting the service and Audrey would be alone in the house for a while yet. Audrey stepped into the room, wondering even as she did why she felt the need to be furtive. She had a greater claim to look through Noah's things than anybody else, surely?

Everything was still neatly folded, the fine wool sweaters, the trousers with their beautiful drape. Looking through his clothes, she wondered how much her attraction to him had been about the way he seemed to get everything right – perfect body, perfect wardrobe, perfect job, perfect taste. If someone like that wants me... she thought. But what did she want? She liked Noah, he matched her idea of what her life should be, but he hadn't stirred her deeply. She hadn't been kissing him hungrily less than twenty-four hours after they met, for example. And how far had her idea of what her life should be really got her? She'd been heading towards the opposite of where she came from for so long. It had worked well enough as an escape route, but now she wanted to be happy. And that meant admitting that the gap between her idea of Noah and the way he made her feel was probably too wide to bridge. In the end, they were only good on paper.

There it was, the thing she'd been waiting for since they set off on this ill-starred trip: clarity. But of course Noah wasn't there to share it with. Poor guy, he was in a fix she couldn't get him out of. She wasn't sure when they'd get to have this conversation.

Then, replacing a sweater in his bag, Audrey found a small pile of letters tucked into its folds. Three of them, open, addressed to Noah. She knew she shouldn't. But how could she not? She pulled the first one an inch out of its envelope, just enough to see that it began:

My son,
  Imagine how it feels to write those words.

She knew! Audrey stood stunned, the past two days running through her head. Why on earth had the two of them play-acted in front of her? Why had Noah brought her along? If this was a reunion of mother and son, their behaviour and her own presence were completely bewildering. But one thing was clear: his lies to her had been bigger than she'd understood. She'd been feeling sympathy for him, the slightly condescending tenderness of the one who leaves towards the one who is left. But now she was angry.

Then another thought emerged from the swirl: if Stella knew who Noah was when they arrived, it can't have been learning the truth that had sent her over the edge of despair. The suicide theory was less credible than ever. Unless… There was that heated discussion she had heard.

She remembered the aborted search of their things before they'd left Trevennick House on the night of Stella's death. DI Morgan had been so busy protecting her honour from Varley's prying eyes that they hadn't gone through their bags properly. The police might never have seen the letters. And if Noah hadn't wanted to tell them they were here, did that mean he was guilty? It definitely meant something. But she couldn't quite see what.

Audrey was about to extract the letter from the envelope, to read more and see what it revealed, when the kitchen door opened and Lamorna called out, 'Duty done! You ready? We'd better get going if you want to catch that train.'

She hesitated, wondering whether to take the letters, to do something with them. But no. She had decided he wasn't her concern. Innocent or guilty, Noah would have to take his chances getting out of this mess. Let him point the police towards the letters, if he thought it would help. She was leaving it behind, all of it: the watchful village, the menacing river, the snakes and the shadows in the trees. The dead, too. Any regrets were ghosts, traces left by the strong emotion of the past two days. They'd fade soon enough. 'Coming!' she called out, and ran down the stairs to the car.

Audrey threw her bag in the back seat, already a jumble of totes filled with things that might be for a church fete or might be for the dump. She paused, her hand on the window frame of the open car door, looking around at the sun-kissed greenery, the dark yews of the churchyard and the vivid beech hedges. The birdsong sounded insistent and querulous, like the birds too were tired of the heat. Or like they were searching for their lost companions, pinioned to the garden hedge.

The vicar appeared from around the side of the rectory, carrying an obby oss and leaning to one side against the weight. Audrey frowned, not best pleased to be seeing another one. She couldn't tell exactly what it was – a chimera, bits of bird and snake and ram all joined together.

'Have to drop this by the green on our way. Bad luck to leave stragglers.' She tossed it in the boot and they got in.

Audrey could smell the sun-warmed wood, in among the staler notes of a little-cleaned car. 'It's too bad you're not staying to see the end of the ritual,' said Lamorna, pulling out into the lane. 'But I suppose, after everything that's happened, you must be eager to leave.'

'You're carrying on? In spite of the deaths?'

'Oh yes. The river has taken its due. Now it's our turn to take something back.'

The vicar pulled up by the green and Audrey waited in the car while she got out and dragged the obby oss into place. There were a few people milling about, but the atmosphere seemed more subdued and less surreal than yesterday. Turning her head, she caught sight of the pub sign, Morwenna's calm, painted gaze hanging in the air next to the vine-covered wall. There was a window among the vines, too, glinting in the sun. She remembered whose room lay behind it and turned away quickly. Just another memory. It would fade. Though she'd never had much success forgetting things she didn't want to remember.

Lamorna returned and they were off, away from the whitewashed cottages and stone-walled farmhouses of the village, through the tree-covered hollow ways, out of that particular fold of country and heading towards the station. Audrey resisted the urge to look back.

The station was different today. When they'd first arrived, Audrey had felt they were slipping back in time – the woods had looked like Sleeping Beauty's forest, both magical and threatening. Now the place was rammed with cars and bag-laden holidaymakers, loud and bright. Lamorna nosed in slowly, trying to drop Audrey right by the entrance, then realised her mistake as other cars filed in behind her – the wait in the exit lane looked eternal. Lamorna would be a long time making it home.

'Sorry,' said Audrey. 'Hopefully this is the last time I cause you trouble.'

'Don't worry,' said Lamorna, 'I'll just park and get a coffee. I'm sure it'll ease off once the train has come and gone.'

They walked onto the platform together. Lamorna was turning towards the cafe steps, which went up to the little hut above the platform. Audrey had to cross the bridge to the other side, and was glad to have a reason to bid her goodbye without going in – Griffin might be manning the cafe again, though she couldn't see from down here.

'Well, I guess this is it,' Audrey said, gesturing around with her duffel bag. 'Thanks again, and sorry for all the hassle.'

'Don't mention it.' Lamorna stood still, waiting.

Audrey felt there ought to be more to say, but perhaps there wasn't. After all, Lamorna had signed up for a life of service and good works; dropping a relative stranger at the station can't have been the most onerous duty she'd ever performed. It felt odd to say goodbye without acknowledging the confidences that had passed between them – or at least from Lamorna to her – but then that was what Audrey wanted, wasn't it? To leave this place and its dramas behind; to be treated as a stranger, not as someone who was involved. She nodded again and began hauling her bag up the steps of the footbridge.

At the bottom, on the other side, she edged around the other passengers waiting for the London train, feeling very single and very silent among the chatting groups of sun-burned travellers. She found a clear space by a pansy-filled planter where she could deposit her bag, and reached for her phone, thinking to check her email, before she remembered there wasn't any service here. But in the end the signal didn't matter.

'Audrey? Oh my God! It *is* you!'

She turned, astonished to be recognised, dreading confirmation that the voice belonged to who she thought it did. But there on the platform, surrounded by children and overstuffed tote bags, was the woman whose messages she'd been ducking for weeks: Jemima. Jemima who was waiting on her illustrations. Illustrations she'd made zero progress on since the last time they spoke.

Audrey opted for a bright, enthusiastic greeting, and hoped against hope it would fend off any questions about blown deadlines. 'Hi! Jemima, wow! What are you doing here?'

'Oh, you know...' Jemima waved at her assembled family – a number of children Audrey couldn't quite pin down, but certainly more than two, were chirping and milling about her husband, who was doling out snacks from a plastic shopping bag. The bridge of his nose was pink, and he was too harassed to acknowledge Jemima's introductory gesture at Audrey. Jemima, too, looked rumpled and a little used up by the heat. 'I've been trying to get in touch with you, did you get my emails?'

'Service down here is terrible, sorry.'

'I thought you were going to Paris for the weekend.'

She seized on the potential excuse. 'I was meant to, but I thought I'd do a last bit of research, you know, fill the well and immerse myself in the countryside. It's been incredibly helpful. But here I am, going on. I don't want to fill your holidays with work!'

Audrey thought she might cry if she didn't even get a train journey's worth of peace between the frying pan of events in Trevennick and the fire of what was waiting for her back home. She tried to fend off the inevitable book query with questions of her own.

'How's it been, did you have a nice time?'

'Nice enough, but too much of it. It's not even the school holidays yet. We came down for my parents' ruby wedding, it was only meant to be a couple of days away. But we've been stuck here since Friday night. It's turned into a real nightmare, we had to extend our booking and next week's going to be horrible, trying to catch up on what I've missed.'

'Oh no. What happened?' Audrey was barely listening; she kept looking around for an escape route, although there was none, and they were bound to sit near each other on the train. But the longer she could keep Jemima talking about her travel woes instead of missed deadlines, the better.

'All the trains were stopped after that big storm. Didn't you hear about the washed-out tracks? You must have come down before then, otherwise you would have got my messages. I've been trying to check in on your progress.'

Jemima's tone was good-humoured enough under her exhaustion, but she wasn't going to be put off. Audrey's heart sank, and she started preparing an explanation of why the illustrations weren't ready, how quickly she could do them, why it was actually a very good thing, because she'd had a chance to refresh her eyes and she had a completely new perspective, which would make for an even better— but then her brain snagged on something Jemima had said.

'You mean since the storm on Friday night?'

'Yes.'

'All the trains? Cancelled?'

'Yes. You know the bit by the sea at Dawlish, where it runs close to the water?' Audrey remembered the remarkable prospect, and remembered thinking that the waves must get awfully close in a storm. 'A bit of the sea wall failed, and the county's been cut off for more than a day. This is the first train back. Why do you think it's so crowded?'

'You're sure? There were no trains running yesterday morning? In either direction?'

The other woman cocked her head and stared at her, clearly wondering whether something had broken in Audrey's brain. 'I'm sure,' she repeated slowly. 'We've been waiting for a train home since yesterday.'

'Jemima, I'm so sorry. I have to go. I promise I'll email about the pictures. Have a good journey home!' Audrey heaved her bag over her shoulder and started pushing through the crowd to get back to the stairs, ignoring the woman calling after her.

She knew who had killed DI Morgan.

CHAPTER 21

Across the bridge and down the other side she went, her bag bumping against her hip. She rushed up the stairs of the cafe on the other platform. Her mind was full of her realisation, but there was a corner reserved for her own concerns – in that small space she had room to be relieved Lamorna was coming out of the door with a cardboard cup and she wouldn't have to go in and face Griffin.

'Lamorna! I know I said this was the last time I'd put you out, but I need a lift. We have to go to the police.'

'Slow down.' The vicar pulled her out of the way of someone trying to get into the cafe, and walked her gently down the stairs to the bottom. Audrey chafed at the delay.

'I'm sorry, I know it sounds strange, but can we please just go? I'll explain in the car.'

Lamorna gave her a long and searching look, there at the bottom of the stairs, but then gave a grimacing smile and nodded. 'And here I was expecting to drink a leisurely coffee. But I suppose a Sunday is when a vicar should be hard at work.'

Back to the car, flinging her bag in among the rest in the back seat. The same smell of dusty sun-heated fabric and petrol. They joined the exit queue, and Audrey groaned. But now the line was moving, albeit slowly. Looking over to the platform she saw why: the London train had just pulled in. She looked away before she could see it pull out. She had something more important to do, but she didn't like watching her train home disappear.

They were on the main road soon enough, and Lamorna was pressing her for details. 'What's so urgent that we have to go to the police?'

'I know what happened to Paul Morgan.'

Lamorna's eyes flicked over to her, but she looked back at the road quickly. 'What happened, then?'

'Well, I already knew part of it – I tried to explain to Sergeant Varley at the scene, but he wouldn't listen. Someone impersonated Morgan. It stands to reason that that person killed him too.'

'How did you know that?'

'It was my drawing. If I show you…' She turned to the back seat to rummage in her bag, but it was just out of reach. 'I'll show you later. But I could tell they had different postures, bodies – the man wearing DI Morgan's jacket at the river wasn't him. Only no one noticed, because of the mask.'

Lamorna nodded slowly, changing lanes and taking it in. 'Okay. But you knew this already. Sergeant Varley said it didn't stand up. What changed at the station? Why the rush?'

Audrey took a breath. She hadn't put her realisation into words yet. She hoped it would make more sense, and be better received, than what she'd tried to explain yesterday. 'I knew someone must have impersonated him. But Varley didn't want to take the evidence of my pictures, and I had no idea who it could have been, so last night… I'm ashamed to say I told myself I must be wrong. But on the platform, I realised who the murderer is. And that I wasn't wrong at all.'

Lamorna looked over at her. 'Well?'

'Cameron Grant. He killed DI Morgan. I wouldn't be surprised if we learned that somehow he killed Stella Penrose too. I don't know how. And I don't know why. But I'm sure it was him in Morgan's jacket.'

A turning off the main road was coming up, and Lamorna took it. She slowed the car at the first passing place, drawing up under the shade of a tree growing by the hedge. She braked and seemed to be thinking, her gaze turned inward. Perhaps she was reviewing the events of the last two days in her mind. Audrey held her breath, hoping to be believed. Eventually the vicar nodded decisively and said, 'Right.'

Audrey exhaled in relief as they pulled out again. She expected Lamorna to turn back to the main road, but she continued along the lane. Audrey didn't recognise it immediately, not knowing the area, but soon she realised they were retracing the route from the village. 'Shouldn't we be going to Falmouth?' she asked. 'Noah's being held there. I have to explain it to the police. This might help get him out.'

An hour ago, leaving the house, she had been prepared to leave Noah to his fate. But now she was sure someone else was responsible, she had to clear his name.

Lamorna didn't answer directly. 'What makes you so sure it's Cameron who was impersonating Paul at the river?'

'Something I heard on the train platform. The tracks were washed out after the storm, everything after Dawlish was cut off. That's why it was so crowded. People got stuck down here and were all trying to catch the first train back east.'

'Why does that matter?'

'Because Cameron was meant to be on his stag do in Brighton on Friday night. He said he took the train back on Saturday morning. But he couldn't have. The trains weren't running. He's lying. I don't think he left.'

They were passing the occasional house, empty fields, stretches where the woods came up to the road. There were plenty of passing places and tracks off the lane, but Lamorna made no move to turn the car around.

'All right. But how does that connect him to Paul Morgan and the river? We all saw him in his own clothes, there at the ritual like the rest of us.'

'I know, and I didn't suspect anything because I didn't have a reason to be suspicious of him. But once I realised he'd lied about his whereabouts on the night of Stella's death, it made sense – it's always the husband! Or the soon-to-be husband. I don't know how he pulled the trick, but, thinking about the posture and size of the man who was pretending to be DI Morgan, it's got to be him.'

Lamorna was nodding along, listening. She didn't look completely unconvinced, but Audrey could sense that the vicar still had holes to pick in her theory. The prospect of yet again not being believed made her feel desperate.

'Look, none of this is conclusive. But so much has happened, and I've caught Cameron in a lie. I just want a chance to lay it out to the police. They can't have checked with the train companies yet or they'd know about the washout. Don't you think I should tell them? Or am I not making sense?'

'No, no, I'm sure you're right. That's why we're going to confront him.'

'Confront Cameron?'

'Yes, we should tell him we know what he's done, and see how he reacts.'

'Lamorna, no. That seems like a crazy way to do it. I'd much rather talk to the police. They might actually be able to do something. This way is… all we do is tip him off. He might be dangerous!'

'We sort out village problems among ourselves,' replied the vicar. 'The river took DI Morgan. It expects us to take control.'

Lord preserve us from true believers, Audrey thought. She tried to be firm. 'Which is what we're doing by going to the police.'

But Lamorna just looked at the road and carried on driving. So firmness hadn't worked. Maybe pleading would.

'Please turn around. I guess it's different for you, you're a moral authority, I can see why you'd want to confront him. But I just want to go to the police and then get the first train out of here.'

A bark of laughter. 'I'm no moral authority. But I know plenty about sin.'

'Lamorna, please.'

The other woman looked over at her, briefly, before turning back to the road. Audrey had seen a light in her eyes – not a righteous, evangelical light. Slyness. That snake-like look she'd noticed in the church. Suddenly, without any concrete reason, Audrey knew her companion was dangerous. 'Turn the car around,' she insisted. The vicar's hands tightened around the wheel. 'Lamorna! Turn the car around!'

Lamorna pressed a button on the dashboard. With a thunk, the little nub indicating the door's lock position slammed down. Realisation hit Audrey, along with fear. It was so stupid. Despite all the mystical trappings of this village, it boiled down to something so human. So grubby and messy.

'Is it because Trevor was sleeping with Stella?'

The other woman looked over, her face a snarl of bitter humiliation.

If Audrey had stopped to think, she probably wouldn't have done what she did next. But inside her the storm of tension and misery and fear built up over the past few days was breaking. She couldn't think. She could only act.

There was a turning coming up, a little downhill from where they were, with wooden fences and empty fields on either side of it. She grabbed the wheel and wrenched it over.

Lamorna screamed and tried to wrench it back.

The car, already going fast down the hill, swerved and burst through one of the fences, rocketing over the bumpy ground of the field.

Now they were both screaming.

They didn't have time to slow down before they hit the tree.

*

Audrey blinked. Something had happened. Her vision was black – no, it was clearing, there was something running over her eyes, hard to see around, but it was beautiful out there. A tree. Blue sky. Perfect summer sun. Much nicer than the dream she'd been having. She was glad now to realise it was just a dream. Animals chasing her – wooden animals? Things were lurking in the forest, dark things, things that wanted her gone. She'd fallen into the river. That was even darker. She hated the dark. She felt much better, lying here – or was she sitting? – looking at the beautiful bright light. Although everything looked sort of shattered, the tree and the field and the lovely sky. Could the world shatter?

She tried to wipe away whatever was over her eyes, to see more clearly, and her hand came away red. Another bad sign. She needed help.

Audrey looked around. It hurt to turn her head. There was a woman dressed in black, standing with her back to the car. If she could just get her attention.

But although she scratched weakly at the door, trying to open it and get out, the woman didn't turn. Maybe she couldn't hear. Audrey tried to call to her, but it was difficult to control her voice, as well as her limbs.

Someone was walking towards them. She couldn't see his face, but his blonde hair was like a torch in the sunlight. He was facing her. He'd notice. He would help. He had something in his hand, a tool. He was coming to release her.

Then he got closer, and she saw who he was, and the jumbled jigsaw in her mind began to sort itself out. She scrabbled away from the door, struggling with her seat belt, her fingers disobedient.

Cameron wrenched open the door and raised the crowbar above his head.

Audrey was back in the river.

In the black.

CHAPTER 22

It was dark when she woke up. Not here, not here. She couldn't bear it if he left her in there again. Not even a crack of light made it around the cupboard door. Soon things would start moving invisibly around her. She wanted to beg, or to cry out. It was pointless to do either. He would only leave here there longer if she screamed. But she couldn't help it – the scream was going to claw its way out of her throat. She could feel it rising.

Something scraped its way through the blackness towards her. She screamed.

Only a tiny croak came out. Her voice was rasped to nothing. Everything hurt. He must have hit her this time, before he locked her in. She tried to move, to rub her head, but she felt stuck.

Then a little light showed, low down, and she turned towards it in desperation.

Not stuck, tied. Her hands were in the process of being tied. Cameron was tying her up, while Lamorna held a torch, its beam pointing downwards.

She wasn't at home. She wasn't a child being locked in the cupboard by her father. Relief washed over her, but it turned quickly back to cold fear. She might not be trapped in her own particular nightmare, but the situation wasn't good.

'What are you doing?' It came out quiet and slurred. Shit, she probably had a concussion on top of everything else.

Lamorna pointed the torch straight in Audrey's eyes. It hurt like a stab wound. Then it occurred to her that she might be about to find out what a stab wound actually felt like, and she was suddenly a lot less worried about the concussion.

'She's awake.'

Cameron didn't respond at first, just yanked the knots tighter, testing their strength. She could feel that the skin of her wrists was already chafed raw. When he'd finished he straightened and looked down at her. His face was flat, expressionless. She couldn't read what he was thinking, though the context pointed to something... not good. She tried to clear her throat and ask what they were going to do with her, but with her head throbbing from both fear and pain, it was hard to speak.

'Let's give her some water,' said Lamorna. Her voice was gentle, not vindictive. Maybe her plans for Audrey weren't fatal.

Cameron took the torch while Lamorna held a plastic bottle to Audrey's lips. The water didn't go down easy, coming out too fast and making her cough and splutter. 'Thank you,' she said, when the coughing had subsided. Her voice was still a rasp, but it came out clearly enough.

They didn't seem to have any other immediate plans, just stood there looking at her in the unsteady light of the torch beam. Darting her eyes from side to side, Audrey tried to decipher her surroundings in the half-dark. The torch provided most of the light, but there did seem to be a faint grey patch in the distance away to the right, like daylight was waiting somewhere. There was a lot of damp stone, and some actual puddles flashing the torchlight back to her. Her feet seemed to be in one. She dragged them out, feeling the wetness that had already soaked through her trainers.

'Are we in a tunnel?' Audrey asked in her husky, damaged voice. It seemed best to avoid questions that might have unwanted answers, like *What are you going to do with me?*

Lamorna looked at Cameron, evidently seeking approval. He shrugged, like it didn't matter whether the vicar answered her or not. It couldn't be a good sign that they weren't worried about what information they shared.

'It goes into the cliff off the river. The county's full of them, if you know where to look,' said Lamorna, speaking with a certain bookish enthusiasm, as though they were just two history nerds having a chat about local topography. 'Mining tunnels, smuggler's tunnels.'

Audrey thought of the prints she'd seen hanging in Stella's house and in the pub. Men in stocking caps, smugglers, tippling around barrels. A notion was forming at the back of her mind, but she couldn't grasp it. Her head hurt – everything hurt – but at least she was thinking clearly again, if a bit slowly. Had the second bash to her head straightened things out in there? That seemed medically unlikely. How long had she been unconscious? Maybe she'd been out for hours and her brain had had time to grow less confused. That daylight off to the right might not even be from the same day.

'What time is it?'

Lamorna checked her watch in the torch beam. 'Teatime. You must be hungry.' She didn't look like she was about to go and grab her a snack.

Again Audrey held herself back from asking what she really wanted to know: what was going to happen to her? She groped around internally for other ways to keep them talking, other things to ask. Everything carried a danger with it; anything might set off a chain reaction that ended with her not merely tied up and headsore but banished to a much more permanent darkness than that held by this tunnel.

Although it was dark enough. When she'd woken up, childhood monsters she hadn't seen in years had started taking shape in the murk. The beam of the torch hadn't dispelled them. There they were, just beyond hearing, just past the edge of vision, dragging their claws against the stone and slithering towards her. Her heart was going too fast, and her breath too. She was sweating despite the chill underground air, and it was hard to think.

But she had to, if she was going to have any chance of getting out of here. Audrey focused on the beam of torchlight, the faint grey patch off to the right. She felt her back against the wet roughness of the stone wall. To keep them talking, she found a question – perhaps the riskiest one of all.

'You killed Stella Penrose, didn't you?'

Quickly, almost as an involuntary reflex, Lamorna clicked off the torch and then on again. It was very frightening while it was completely dark. Audrey's heartbeat seemed to echo off the tunnel walls. Lamorna was looking at the ground now, her face tilted away.

Cameron took a step towards Audrey, his shoes scraping loudly against the rock floor. He grabbed her by the hair. She gasped as he wrenched her head back and it hit the tunnel wall. He stared at her fixedly. In the low light she could see glints from his eyes, which seemed to go too long without blinking, like a reptile's.

Then he let her go, as roughly as he'd grabbed her, making her bounce painfully against the wall again.

'It was the only way to save the land.'

Audrey waited. She was afraid of him. He had already knocked her out with a crowbar. He had killed. She was in a dark tunnel in a country backwater. She hated the dark. She hadn't formed many opinions on tunnels in her life so far, but if she survived this she didn't think she'd be seeking them out very often in future. If she had a future.

And yet some reserve of pride prevented her from begging, or from looking away. She had spent too many years begging her father, when she should have stared him down. Shamed him. Well, if she was going to die, she would do it as she should have lived. She pressed her back harder into the wet wall and stared at Cameron, challenging him to confess to her direct gaze. She asked the question she'd been avoiding.

'You're going to kill me, aren't you?'

Lamorna turned her whole body away this time. Cameron half-smiled, and knelt in front of Audrey. She wished she could retreat further into the wall, but it was cold and unyielding. He shone the light of his torch straight into her eyes. It was agony, but she didn't blink. He doesn't want to meet my eyes either, she thought. If dying was her only option now, she was going to do it with dignity. 'The tide will rise and wash you away,' he said. He looked around and patted the damp stone walls with a satisfied air. 'This land has already endured so much. The mining, the smuggling, the building. Again and again it's been violated for our greed. Together we're going to give something back.'

'I already have given something back, actually. I'm the illustrator of an urgent and enchanting book about extinct species,' replied Audrey, her jaw tight with the effort of being flippant to her murderer's face. The murderer himself snorted.

'You're a hypocrite. We all are. People. What's the line? Just a virus with shoes. You think what I've done is terrible, and maybe it is, but everywhere we go, terrible things follow. The difference is, I'm doing wrong to set things right.'

Audrey thought of his hectic eyes when she'd seen him on his way to the woods – on his way, she realised now, to kill Paul Morgan. She couldn't see him now, he'd retreated behind the blinding torch beam, but she imagined he looked much the same. There was an evangelical fervour in his voice. Lamorna had evidently heard some of this before; she sighed and went over to the opposite side of the tunnel, taking a seat against the wall, settling in for the recitation. The torch beam bounced and wandered as she moved. Cameron waited for it to settle before he spoke.

CHAPTER 23

'Stella and I decided to get married because – well, for a lot of reasons. It really pains me, knowing we'll never share a bed again. We were the perfect union. Masculine and feminine. Earth and sky. Fire and water.'

Vain and deluded, thought Audrey.

'But it wasn't simply a physical connection. We had the same vision, a dream of a better world. And we were going to make it. Here. She was always talking about Romans and the tin trade, but I think you have to look further back to find the real golden age. It's somewhere back beyond human records. When we lived as one with the land, just animals, like any others roaming these hills, dying and being reabsorbed into the woods, the fields, the water, the soil. That's how things should be.'

He looked down at his hands. It was hard to read his expression in the glancing light, but Audrey thought she saw hatred for himself there, for everything a human hand can represent.

'The world humanity has made is filthy and grey – concrete, car exhaust, rivers you can't swim in. And that's what most people want, to keep spreading the taint. When I came here and saw how they'd kept some of the old ways alive, I thought maybe, just maybe, they got it. That this was a part of the world I could restore, I could protect. And when I met Stella, it was like a place had been waiting for me. Like I'd been called. The work I was always meant to do, the woman I was meant to do it with.'

There was nothing funny about her position, but Audrey almost smiled at the symmetry. Herself, fleeing a country childhood to make a city life; Cameron, fleeing the city's taint to make a country self. It was good she suppressed the urge, because he continued to speak in a voice full of anger.

'I couldn't give it up without a fight.'

He looked at her like he expected her to say something. He waited, his gaze directed at her in all its intensity, burning through the dark. Eventually she said, 'I wasn't trying to take it away from you.'

He let out a bitter huff of laughter. 'Not you. Your boyfriend.'

'We sort of broke up.'

Cameron laughed, a giggle that frightened her as much as the dark or the crowbar. 'Oh well then, let's untie you and get you out of here.'

She let his laughter pass before asking, 'How could he have been in your way? He just wanted to get to know his mother.'

'Wrong place, wrong time. Stella and I were about to change everything around here – rewilding the land, restoring what had been lost. She owns all those acres up by her house. We were going to introduce beavers, we were about to create a trust that would preserve her land, make sure it was never developed. We would keep living in the house, do the work, be stewards, and then be returned to the soil when we died.'

There was the fervour again, and his eyes seemed to shine a little more in the darkness. Audrey had no desire to live anywhere that could be described as wild, and the fixation on dead bodies being worked back into the life cycle was creepy. But she recognised vision when she saw it. Ambition. He'd been about to launch the project of his life. It wasn't about money, it was about meaning. This was everything to Cameron, she could tell.

'Until she got a message from the adoption agency she'd used when she was young, telling her that her son had been enquiring about his origins and might want to be in touch. Then suddenly she was slowing down our plans. Then came the talk about her "legacy". What legacy could be more important than healing the earth? She was even talking about using some of the land for a development, to build houses, so she could leave this son she'd never even met more assets. I realised… I realised she'd never been the person I thought she was.'

Audrey thought this was probably true. She had only known Stella for an evening, but she hadn't struck her as someone who'd find the idea of dissolving back into the soil all that compelling. Too much ego. Whatever she did, she'd want credit for it. 'We can let our hopes run away with us when we're in love,' she said. 'We all idealise people.'

As soon as she had spoken, Audrey could see that it was a mistake – no bid to humanise herself, to build a connection with her captor, was going to work. He looked at her with a kind of sarcastic half-smile, as though he could read her attempt perfectly clearly and found it pathetic. 'You idealised that guy? Noah? Lamorna can commiserate with you, she's got terrible taste in men.' He shifted to look at the vicar leaning against the tunnel wall behind him.

'Don't.' Lamorna's reply was spoken in a low voice, calmer than Cameron's, but there was a vehemence and a force to it that Audrey took note of. Maybe that was a thread she could pull. Lamorna had her own reasons for getting involved; they might not align perfectly with Cameron's.

Audrey felt the knots in the thin cord that bound her wrists, hoping for a more literal thread to pull. She was tied tightly; her hands hurt, straining against the strict ligature and bending into awkward shapes as they groped after a loose end. She was worried her fingers would soon go completely numb.

Cameron stood and began pacing back and forth, his ankles kicking through Lamorna's torch beam, his face out of view. 'We had plans, perfect plans. And then this long-lost son pops up. And suddenly Stella changes her tune. Now she doesn't want to leave the earth healthier when she goes, she wants to leave some strange guy richer. I couldn't let her. This opportunity wouldn't happen again. So she had to go. She had to go.'

He stopped as he said this the second time, directly in front of Audrey, leaning down and spitting the words into her face. She remembered her father saying things like this – *Look what you made me do.* Why did awful men always want you to agree they were right to be awful? She was sick of it. She wanted to lock Cameron in a cupboard and walk away. Let him justify himself to the things that lived in the dark. Unfortunately, she was in no position to turn the tables. Her fingers were aching and exhausted, and she hadn't found any weak points in the knots. She needed to keep him talking.

'I see why you did it. But I still don't see how.'

'Ah.' There was relish in his voice now. They were getting to the part he was proud of. 'Who do they always look at first, when someone's murdered? Lamorna?'

She cleared her throat and said wearily, 'The husband.'

'Exactly. And if I was suspected, then the land would be lost anyway, and there wouldn't have been any point. So I had to muddy the waters, didn't I? Didn't I?'

It wasn't clear whose affirmation he wanted, but Audrey stayed silent and let Lamorna give another weary assent. Around the edges of her fear she had room to feel a sort of bored exasperation that she had to sit here listening to this self-justifying twaddle. She could sense Lamorna found it tedious as well.

'The first thing to do,' continued Cameron, 'was to make sure that Noah was here when it happened. If anyone was going to be suspected, I wanted it to be him. He'd written her a letter. And letters are easy to intercept.

'I faked a reply. I didn't give him too much of what he wanted – all that sentimental stuff about reunions and getting to know each other. But enough. I suggested he come to the village for Golowan. I said we could meet then. And I convinced Stella to put the house online for holiday lets.

More revenue. More legacy. More to pass on to the offspring she didn't know I was writing to. That's the trouble with people, isn't it? More. It's always more.

'With only the name of the village to go on, he was bound to stumble on our place. All I had to do was make arrangements, without mentioning Stella, and tell Stella some people would be staying while I was away. It would be a perfectly ironic end. Ships in the night.'

So she hadn't known, thought Audrey. She felt a pang. Perhaps she, too, would die without ever speaking to Noah again, and neither of them would be able to offer the other the explanations and apologies they owed. But she said none of this to Cameron. Instead, she tried to make him spin out his own explanation further, as she again bent her tired fingers to the knots. It would be easier to focus if she closed her eyes. But then she would be in full darkness.

'I'm surprised she agreed to play hostess. If she was so ready to leave everything to you, why would she want to cook dinner for a couple of strangers?'

'Oh, come on. She loved an audience. All I had to tell her was that the two people staying were fans – they'd sought the place out in order to have the honour of meeting her. I knew she'd put on a magnanimous show and welcome you enthusiastically. And then, when she was found dead… muddy waters.'

He was enjoying his narration now. It had taken him a while to get going – until you were caught, you probably didn't get a lot of practice telling the story of your murders. But now that he was in the flow of the tale, he was more and more puffed up, proud of his achievements, his cleverness. He knew he was going to get away with it. Under his voice Audrey could almost hear the inhabitants of the dark, readying themselves for her.

'But how? How do you kill a woman who sleeps in a locked glass bedroom at the top of a cliff?'

'Look around you.' Cameron held out his arms, turning and taking in the tunnel. 'It's coming full circle. The pattern's so beautiful, if you're capable of seeing it.'

'I guess I'm not capable, because I don't see it. She was found in her room, not in a tunnel.'

Cameron didn't respond directly. He turned to Lamorna. She shifted a little where she sat against the tunnel wall, causing the torch to roll on the ground. The beam went spinning around the dark stone space. As she did this, Audrey recognised the knot that bound her, a vague memory drifting up from the Girl Guides days to cause her despair. It was a poacher's knot. Very secure. Not easy to undo. Hence its use by poachers.

Lamorna spoke. 'What you have to understand is… The thing is, Stella's new plans, they would have fouled the river. As a member of the parish council, I'd been working with Stella and Cameron on the rewilding idea. The location of the development, there would have been pipes and waste and things going in. And just at that spot – just at that spot, that's where Trevor has his mussel ropes.'

'She couldn't have that, could she?' There was a curdled amusement in Cameron's voice. 'Nothing must happen to her precious Trevor.'

Audrey didn't bother to point out that his reasons for murder were not really to be preferred. Instead, she directed her remarks at Lamorna: 'But doesn't all this… well, doesn't it go against your vocation?'

Lamorna gave a slightly hollow laugh. 'People who don't believe are always trying to tell those of us who do that we're getting it wrong. Religion isn't a highway code, telling you when you should signal and where you're not allowed to turn. It's a way of naming what's most important in this life. My vocation, since you're so worried about it, is honouring the sacred.'

It looked like an appeal to the Christian value of not murdering people wasn't going to work. Audrey tried sympathy. Maybe this would be a more useful ploy with the vicar than it had been with Cameron. 'So you got involved to protect the man you love?'

'I'd spent enough time with Trevor out on the river to know about the tunnels – smuggling families passed that knowledge down. If you know where to look, you can still get around half the county without having to go above ground.'

'It's true, she was always tagging after him. That's what gave me the idea, seeing them out by the mussel ropes one day,' said Cameron. 'I figured the rich never go without their creature comforts, and the river used to be a route used by those who provided them. So all I had to do to get access was find the place where they ran brandy up to the big house. Lamorna here, once she saw the value of what I was doing, was willing to show me.'

'The tunnel goes up to the house?' asked Audrey.

'It opens at the top of the cliff, where there's just enough room to reach through the open window of the master bedroom, though no one looking out would notice unless you were standing right there. And if you've called someone over to you, someone who knows you, and they come to investigate—'

'You can stab them in the neck,' finished Audrey.

Cameron fell silent, as though even he, grandstanding and spouting his eco-spiritual justifications with evident relish, felt hesitant to talk about the act itself. But he wasn't going to stop running the film. He simply picked up a frame later. 'And if you shut the window, and nobody else knew about the tunnel, whoever discovered them would think they'd done it to themselves.'

Audrey thought about all of this. It was a risk. What if the choreography hadn't gone to plan? What if he hadn't got her? But then, Cameron was a megalomaniac. And in the end it had worked out just as he'd hoped. She remembered the bang that had woken her up, and the sound of footsteps in the empty house. 'I heard you. That night. The window slamming shut and then your footsteps in the tunnel.'

He knelt in front of her, the torch beam carving him into areas of light and shadow. 'The trickiest thing was the timing with the water. You remember the storm that night. Imagine being out on a boat in that weather. And then imagine having to make sure your... activities coincided with low tide. It's an estuary, you know. The water level rises. As I pointed out earlier.'

'People are going to ask where I am.' Audrey wasn't going to be the one to reveal how few people would be interested.

A few emails from Jemima might build up; but she wasn't sure there were many others who would wonder where she'd gone.

'It's a risk we'll have to take. Happily, you've left your possessions with Lamorna. Including that very creepy book of drawings. Really unsettling stuff – you clearly have talent. Talent which will be very helpful in providing a possible motive for your disappearance, should anyone enquire too closely.'

'What a lovely compliment. I'm so gifted that you can pin a murder on me.'

Audrey hadn't been able to bite back the words, but she could see that it had been a mistake. Cameron didn't take kindly to those who compromised his dignity; she thought of his angry refusals of help after Noah had punched him on the green. Now his jaw tightened, and he stood and worked his hands. He seemed to be trying to articulate what she worried were the last words she'd ever hear. There was coiled rage visible all over him, even in the dark, and if she didn't think of something, quickly, maybe he wasn't going to wait for the rising tide to kill her.

'But drawing doesn't make me a murderer. Actually, it helped me figure out who the murderer was. I know you were wearing Paul Morgan's clothes at the river. I could tell from the sketches I did.'

Cameron shrugged. 'So Lamorna said when she called. Clever of you. But I doubt anyone else will see what you saw in those drawings. And nobody will believe they're proof of anything.'

Audrey knew from her attempt to explain to Varley that this was true. She cast around for another angle. How else could she make him keep talking? Just talk, not action. 'But I don't understand how you did it,' she said. 'He was there at the ford, and then he was dead at the foot of the bridge – and in between nobody noticed a thing.'

'They didn't, did they?' mused Cameron. 'I suppose the thing about murder is, you can only learn by doing. You just don't know if you're any good until you try. And once I tried, I knew I had a talent. It was the easiest thing in the world. I met him in the woods on the other side of the river. Lamorna had sent him there, on a wild goose chase. I hit him hard. I stowed the body in the bushes. I came back to town and helped with the statues on the green, made sure everyone saw me there helping all afternoon. It felt...' He groped for the right word, reliving the moment. 'It felt effortless, like I was part of the pattern, like I was the bee and what I had to do was the flower.'

If she hadn't been frightened for her life, Audrey would have rolled her eyes at this lyricism.

'I dressed in his jacket for the Golowan ritual. When you bumped into me I was stowing it in the back of my van. But you didn't notice. I put on the ram's head, and I made an offering in his guise. Lamorna was there at the start, too, it was easy to get ahead of the crowd and pass her the jacket when the others were still caught up at the ford. She climbed out on the woodland side of the river, replaced the jacket on his body and dragged him into the water of the tributary while everyone else was singing and processing. The body got stuck on the bridge, and everyone assumed he slipped and fell. It was too bad about the rigor mortis – if I'd realised that would raise questions, I wouldn't have… prepared him so many hours in advance.'

'But why? He seemed like a kind man.'

Cameron made a disgusted noise, as though it should be obvious. But it was Lamorna who responded.

'He was a detective. Discovery was his business.'

'And he'd discovered what you'd done? How? And how did you know?'

'The bumbling idiot told her. I guess he couldn't look past the dog collar. He thought it was a sign of virtue.' Lamorna shifted against the wall, turning her head away. Ashamed. But if she was also angry…

'So when you spoke in the pub he let out that he knew how Cameron had done it?' asked Audrey.

Lamorna nodded. 'Morgan grew up inland, but farmers were smugglers too, back in the day. One of the pictures in the pub, it made him think. It was just a theory so far, but he was going to confirm it – if you were hunting for it and you kept asking, soon enough you'd find someone in the village who knew where to find this tunnel. But he didn't think it was Cameron who'd killed her.'

Audrey thought. 'Trevor. He'd realised who Stella was sleeping with. And Trevor knows the river.'

'I'd have been happy to let Trevor take the fall,' said Cameron in an idle tone, as though commenting on the weather. 'Trevor or Noah, it didn't matter. The bitch betrayed me for both of them.'

'But you couldn't bear that,' said Audrey to Lamorna, no longer speaking with caution, feeling the momentum of successive revelations driving her on. 'So you insisted that Morgan had to die.'

'She's got you there, padre,' said Cameron.

'He's free now,' whispered the vicar. 'He'll come to me now that he's free.'

Audrey pressed her. 'But what about the next time Trevor pisses Cameron off? He doesn't have very good self-control, does he? I saw you two arguing the day I arrived. He knew you were planning something, didn't he? What happens when he asks questions, and Cameron starts worrying that he isn't going to get away with murder? He might be free, but he isn't safe.'

A silence fell. Tension and attention coursed between the conspirators with the quiet sizzle of an electric circuit about to blow.

'Lamorna and I are in this together,' said Cameron in a measured voice, looking not at Audrey but at the vicar, who was slowly standing up, one hand on the wet wall behind her for support.

'I did all this for Trevor, not for you. For love,' said Lamorna. She shone her torch at Cameron, straight into his face, and he flinched at the brightness, trying to block it with his hand. They stood there, swaying slightly in rhythm with each other, one face lit with an interrogatory beam, one in darkness, both poised for action.

Cameron made up his mind and spoke: 'He's safe as long as he keeps his nose out of it.'

Which proved to be the wrong thing to say. Lamorna leapt at him.

There was never going to be a better moment. Audrey closed her eyes and struggled with the knot. It was very dark. She knew there were things moving in the shadow. But not snakes, or clawed things, or obby osses come to life. Nor even her father. The monsters were two murderers, struggling on the wet stone floor. And Audrey wasn't going to stay in the dark with them.

The thing about a poacher's knot is that, if you want it to be really secure, you have to tie a stopper in the tag end. Otherwise it's possible, if you know what you're dealing with and have a human's dexterity, not a rabbit's, to work that end up and through. And then all you have is an overhand knot, which will come undone by merely looking at it. Or by tugging your hands apart sharply.

Which is exactly what Audrey did.

Once her hands were free, she was away down the tunnel, heading for the faint grey light of the outside world.

CHAPTER 24

Audrey arrived at the mouth of the tunnel with no plan, heart beating a thousand miles an hour, exhilarated by her escape but terrified of what lay behind her.

Cameron and Lamorna didn't immediately appear; they must still be fighting. She wasn't sure she wanted to think about how that might end.

But that didn't mean she was safe: in front of her was a broad expanse of river, with only a small shore sloping up to the mouth of the tunnel and no obvious way across. The river here – past the village proper, as far towards the sea as Stella's house – was much more obviously an estuary than the narrow flow that went through the village. Swimming across would be possible but dangerous. On the other hand, so was waiting here until one of the killers emerged, covered in blood and ready to spill more.

And then, like a miracle, a boat arrived.

Sitting next to the outboard motor and steering was Trevor Kingcup. Standing in the prow, precarious, waving and shouting, was his brother. The dog, too. They both leapt out as the boat bumped against the shore and Griffin took her in his arms while the dog played about their legs. 'Thank Christ,' he said.

She let him hold her, melting into him with relief, but when her heartbeat had slowed a little, she remembered where they had left things and pushed him away.

Now another boat was nosing into the shore, and Varley and another two policemen were jumping out.

'They're in the tunnel,' she said, pointing behind her, and they nodded and ran into the dark.

'Are you all right?' asked Griffin.

'No,' she replied.

Audrey closed her eyes and thought about the place she'd emerged from, and how things had been meant to end there. But she'd saved herself. Once again, she'd had the strength to save herself. And maybe this time she could leave a little more of the past behind.

'I will be, though.'

The police emerged, dragging the murderers with them. Both were flushed, their clothes pulled about, their hair mussed and faces scratched. Cameron wore a small, superior smile and met nobody's eyes. 'Trevor!' Lamorna called out as Varley dragged her into the police boat. 'It was all for you!'

But Trevor didn't look her way. Nor would he meet Audrey's gaze as he steered the boat back to the village.

Shouting to be heard above the motor, Griffin explained. 'I… I noticed you at the station.' He looked embarrassed, like it cost him something to admit he'd been watching for her. 'I knew you couldn't wait to get out of here, and then when you turned around and left in a hurry, something felt wrong.'

He'd asked his brother to look out for the vicar and Audrey returning to the village, and his brother had come clean about a few things: the affair with Stella, for one, and the fact that Lamorna had told him she had a way to stop Stella poisoning his mussels. No one knew the river better than Trevor; when he'd understood how far things had gone – when Griffin explained that there were reasons to think both recent deaths had been unnatural – he knew to take them to the tunnel.

Audrey listened and looked at Trevor sitting at the other end of the boat, shamefaced and no doubt glad of the noise to cover his brother's narration. He wasn't a murderer himself, but he'd known enough to bear some responsibility. He'd have questions to answer when they reached the shore. Still, she felt a little shamefaced herself when she remembered all the times she'd taken his moodiness for murderous intent. The argument with Lamorna, his angry remarks at the pub, his rough handling of her when she tried to show Varley her sketches – he had some cobwebby corners in his soul that needed sweeping out. But he wasn't a killer.

Perhaps that was why it seemed safe enough to accept his mother's offer of a room for as long as it was needed. She couldn't leave yet; the police had to clear things up.

'You'd better have that break you came down here for,' said Morwenna, making up a bed for her. 'It's not such a bad place when people aren't busy killing each other.'

*

Now Audrey was watching the bonfire that marked the end of the Golowan celebrations. The flames leapt red and orange and white against the deepening blue of the evening sky. Smoke rose up, occasionally blowing into the crowd and provoking coughs and laughter. They were all there, the whole village, burning the obby osses. The atmosphere was much looser than it had been at the river: people passed wry comments on proceedings as they darted forward to toss another woven animal on the flames. Drinks were handed out and everyone complained good-humouredly about the heat of the fire on this already hot day. They were all gathered to witness the end, and Audrey was among them.

Noah was there too – he'd been released as soon as the police called in their arrest of Cameron and Lamorna. He was innocent of murder. He might be guilty of assault, but in the circumstances it seemed unlikely Cameron would be pressing charges.

They stood together at the edge of the green, waiting for a car which would take Noah away to a nearby hotel. He had to hang around for a few days, too. They traded awkward smiles, both feeling they ought to talk but not sure what to say. Eventually Audrey pointed at his bag and said, 'I see you got your stuff back. Sorry I kind of left it with a murderer.'

'You weren't to know,' he said, but he was half-smiling. The past couple of days seemed to have knocked a little of the stiffness out of him. Then his face grew sad. 'Besides, it's just clothes – the letters were the only thing that mattered to me in there, and it turns out they didn't mean what I thought they did. They've taken them as evidence, anyway.'

'I'm glad you're not in jail.'

'If it weren't for you, I might be. Look, I'm sorry about everything that happened. I brought you down here because… I don't know, I didn't know I was going to meet her, the whole thing with the house was crazy. But I thought I might bump into her by chance, and I wanted to give a certain impression of how I was doing in life, you know? A beautiful girlfriend was part of that. But it wasn't right, keeping you in the dark, using you. I'd understand if you hated me.'

Audrey was quiet, considering. Now it was her turn. To do the right thing. To say what she felt. To bring her heart out of the darkness, into the light. 'It wasn't totally fair. But then, neither was continuing the relationship when I knew I didn't love you.' His startled eyes met hers. She took a breath and carried on. 'To be clear, since we've neither of us been great at that so far, I'm breaking up with you.'

They both smiled, their expressions frank and full of goodwill.

'Thanks for the clarity,' he said. 'Though I'd given up expecting us to survive this weekend.'

'As a couple? Or literally?'

He gave a rueful laugh, and then sorrow settled back over his face.

'I'm sorry you didn't get a chance to know your mother,' she said.

'Who knows what might have been? I'm not sure what kind of woman she really was. I recognised her straight away – I know you saw that. But she didn't understand who I was, until I told her late that night. Because of the letters,

I thought she knew and was just trying to be discreet around you, wait till we could talk in private before she... acknowledged me. But she hadn't understood, and she was furious, like I'd tricked her. And then I didn't say anything to anybody later because I thought what I'd told her had made all this happen. I thought she killed herself because of me. I was so busy feeling guilty, I didn't even try to piece things together. Because of me, the people responsible almost got away.'

For a heartbeat, his face was utterly desolate. Then he gave her a making-the-best-of-it half-smile and nodded to where the Kingcup brothers were talking to each other.

'But I found family, of a sort. If they want to know me. And... a friend?' This was for her, and his look was as vulnerable and lovable as she'd ever known.

'A friend,' she said, and stuck her hand out to shake.

He turned to go; his car had arrived. But he paused at the open door and said, 'You know, the stuff you've been drawing down here – I peeked into your sketchbook – it's really good. Dark. But good. We should talk about it someday. When we're both back home.'

'Thanks, but I've got a commission to finish first,' she said. 'The countryside is turning out to be a more interesting subject than I thought.'

They nodded at each other, and waved as the car pulled away.

Griffin was waiting to speak to her, looking a little warm from the fire. Or was it nerves? 'All okay?'

She nodded.

'We're friends. And you have a brother, if you want him.'

'I do, but…' Griffin reached up a hand to ruffle the hair at the back of his head, uncertain. 'Not if it means missing my shot with you.'

'Oh really?'

Audrey looked away at the fire, the gathered villagers, this place that had frightened her and nearly killed her but which had also made her stronger. This was where she'd buried the past, finally. It made a backwards sort of sense. She looked back at Griffin. He had offended and infuriated her from the start; but he had understood her, too, and thrilled her, and made her think about how good life could be, even a small, unglamorous, provincial life, if it was lived among people who cared about you.

'I have my whole life in the city, you know. My work.'

He nodded and fell back a step, ready to take it as a rejection, ready to leave her alone. Forever, maybe.

'But I hear you've got Wi-Fi in this village now.'

The beginnings of his crooked smile. 'Oh yeah. We're pretty up to date.'

'For the late twentieth century, anyway.'

It was a full grin now. He took her in his arms. It was hard to tell whether the heat and the glow came from the fire or from his body. She kissed him back, and concluded it didn't matter. Either way, it was the warmth of home.

ACKNOWLEDGEMENTS

My thanks to Mark Richards and Clare Conville for another ride on the carousel. To Alex Billington and Sarah Terry for making the inside beautiful, and to Holly Ovenden for doing the same to the outside. To the Cornish National Music Archive, for their history of the traditional midsummer bonfire song 'Tansys Golowan'; I have used the version collected in the 1920s by Ralph Dunstan as my epigraph. To Jack Ramm, for his generosity with time and ideas. To Ari Aster for showing how to find darkness in bright summer light. To Daphne du Maurier for writing about Cornwall better than I ever could, and to the Smith-Laing clan for moving there, without which I wouldn't have written about it at all. To Joel Klenck for taking pleasure in a good mystery. To Valerie Haumont, Ally Marks and Julien Scherliss for many discussions of the artistic process. To Alicia Marie and Tess Lorraine for having much faith. To Tim, for absolutely everything. And to Redmond, for waiting to be born until I'd finished the first round of edits, and then taking enough naps that I could finish the rest.